ideals
TRAVEL

There's a call in my heart for the great outdoors;
There's a longing within my breast
To seek the depths of the deepest woods,
Where I find, in their solitude, rest.

There's a charm in the great outdoors for me,
In the music of birds and breeze,
In the soughing pines and the swishing boughs,
The voice and the cry of the trees.

There is ever within me a strong desire
To gaze on the restless sea;
And its rolling waves, and its noisy roar,
Are a soothing tonic to me.

There's a yearning to wander in desert sands;
To pass away lightly the hours,
To inhale the dry air and to feast tired eyes,
On the patches of gay-colored flowers.

There's a cry in my soul of thankfulness,
That I am permitted to see,
To hear and to feel the touch of God,
In the wonders of land and sea.

Agnes Davenport Bond

Publisher, James A. Kuse
Managing Editor, Ralph Luedtke
Editor/Ideals, Colleen Callahan Gonring
Associate Editor, Linda Robinson
Production Manager, Mark Brunner
Photographic Editor, Gerald Koser
Copy Editor, Norma Barnes
Art Editor, Duane Weaver
Contributing Editor, Beverly Wiersum Charette

ISBN 0-89542-333-2

IDEALS—Vol. 37, No. 5 July MCMLXXX. IDEALS (ISSN 0019-137X) is published eight times a year,
January, February, April, June, July, September, October, November
by IDEALS PUBLISHING CORPORATION, 11315 Watertown Plank Road, Milwaukee, Wis. 53201
Second class postage paid at Milwaukee, Wisconsin. Copyright © MCMLXXX by IDEALS PUBLISHING CORPORATION.
All rights reserved. Title IDEALS registered U.S. Patent Office.
Published Simultaneously in Canada.

ONE YEAR SUBSCRIPTION—eight consecutive issues as published—only $15.95
TWO YEAR SUBSCRIPTION—sixteen consecutive issues as published—only $27.95
SINGLE ISSUES—only $2.95

Windmills

The most foreign and picturesque structures on the Cape, to an inlander, not excepting the saltworks, are the windmills—gray-looking, octagonal towers, with long timbers slanting to the ground in the rear, and there resting on a cartwheel, by which their fans are turned round to face the wind. These appeared also to serve in some measure for props against its force. A great circular rut was worn around the building by the wheel. [The windmills] looked loose and slightly locomotive, like huge wounded birds, trailing a wing or a leg, and reminded one of pictures of the Netherlands.

Being on elevated ground, and high in themselves, they serve as landmarks, for there are no tall trees, or other objects commonly, which can be seen at a distance in the horizon; though the outline of the land itself is so firm and distinct, that an insignificant cone, or even precipice of sand, is visible at a great distance from over the sea. Sailors making the land commonly steer either by the windmills, or the meetinghouses. In the country, we are obliged to steer by the meetinghouses alone. Yet the meeting-house is a kind of windmill, which runs one day in seven, turned either by the winds of doctrine or public opinion, or more rarely by the winds of Heaven, where another sort of grist is ground, of which, if it be not all bran or musty, if it be not *plaster*, we trust to make bread of life.

Henry David Thoreau

Robert Louis Stevenson

As a young boy, Robert Louis Stevenson dreamed of becoming a "man of letters," and made a vow early in life that he would learn to write. An only child who possessed a weak disposition and frail body, Stevenson spent most of his youth playing in a fantasy world populated by the adventurous, robust heroes of childhood fables. These stories of his childhood took the lonely, sensitive boy out of himself, as in later years the Scottish author would take countless other children and adults on the same magical flights of fancy. A collection of poems recalling his boyhood experiences are contained in the volume, *A Child's Garden of Verses*, especially in the set subtitled, "The Child Alone." According to his father's wishes, Stevenson was sent to Edinburgh University to study law, but the budding author devoted more time to writing and editing a university magazine than to his studies. After his schooling, Stevenson traveled to France where he met Fanny Osbourne, an American woman who would later become his wife. When the couple married, Fanny was told that her frail, young husband had only months to live. That Stevenson survived for another fourteen years to accomplish his best work was largely due to the devotion, care and self-sacrifice of his wife. Stevenson's major talent lay in his ability to imbue his greatest works, *Treasure Island, Dr. Jekyll and Mr. Hyde,* and *Kidnapped* with both a keen awareness of the supernatural and a lighthearted romanticism, which turned common places and history into poetic, adventurous narrative. By his death in 1894, Stevenson had assured himself a place in English literature and had accomplished far more than his simple desire to "leave an image for a few years upon men's minds."

The Hayloft

Through all the pleasant meadow-side
The grass grew shoulder-high,
Till the shining scythes went far and wide
And cut it down to dry.

These green and sweetly smelling crops
They led in waggons home;
And they piled them here in mountain tops
For mountaineers to roam.

Here is Mount Clear, Mount Rusty-Nail,
Mount Eagle and Mount High;
The mice that in these mountains dwell,
No happier are than I!

Oh, what a joy to clamber there,
Oh, what a place for play,
With the sweet, the dim, the dusty air,
The happy hills of hay.

The Vagabond

Give to me the life I love;
Let the lave go by me;
Give the jolly heaven above
And the byway nigh me.
Bed in the bush with stars to see,
Bread I dip in the river—
There's the life for a man like me,
There's the life forever.

Let the blow fall soon or late;
Let what will be o'er me;
Give the face of earth around
And the road before me.
Wealth I seek not, hope nor love,
Nor a friend to know me;
All I seek, the heaven above
And the road below me.

Or let autumn fall on me
Where afield I linger,
Silencing the bird on tree,
Biting the blue finger.
White as meal the frosty field,
Warm the fireside haven—
Not to autumn will I yield,
Not to winter even!

Let the blow fall soon or late,
Let what will be o'er me;
Give the face of earth around,
And the road before me.
Wealth I ask not, hope nor love,
Nor a friend to know me;
All I ask, the heaven above
And the road below me.

The Gardener

The gardener does not love to talk,
He makes me keep the gravel walk;
And when he puts his tools away,
He locks the door and takes the key.

Away behind the currant row
Where no one else but cook may go,
Far in the plots, I see him dig,
Old and serious, brown and big.

He digs the flowers, green, red, and blue,
Nor wishes to be spoken to.
He digs the flowers and cuts the hay,
And never seems to want to play.

Silly gardener! Summer goes,
And winter comes with pinching toes,
When in the garden bare and brown
You must lay your barrow down.

Well now, and while the summer stays,
To profit by these garden days,
Oh, how much wiser you would be
To play at Indian wars with me!

Farewell to the Farm

The coach is at the door at last;
The eager children, mounting fast
And kissing hands, in chorus sing:
Goodbye, goodbye, to everything!

To house and garden, field and lawn,
The meadow gates we swang upon,
To pump and stable, tree and swing,
Goodbye, goodbye, to everything!

And fare you well for evermore,
O ladder at the hayloft door,
O hayloft where the cobwebs cling,
Goodbye, goodbye, to everything!

Crack goes the whip, and off we go;
The trees and houses smaller grow;
Last, round the woody turn we swing:
Goodbye, goodbye, to everything!

THE SPIRIT OF AMERICA—1980

The spirit of America is showing
   As we travel this land coast to coast.
Our people still stand to honor the flag
   That attests to those freedoms we boast.

Old memories shared are part of it all.
   Men of faith fought and died for its birth.
That spirit, like bugle notes played from the heart,
   Is sounding our anthem all over the earth.

Fifty states, individually united,
   Have a strength that withstands every test.
Tempests rage, protests march in their season—
   United we stand for the right and the best.

America is more than possessions.
   Back in history her saga begins.
Strife and struggle add strength to her lessons
   That are based on faith, family and friends.

From each city, village, town, every suburb—
   All over this land far and wide,
The spirit of America is growing,
   Where the people choose God as their guide.

Alice Leedy Mason

This beautiful painting by John Slobodnik is featured on Ideals' special patriotic issue, **The Spirit of America**. For ordering information, please turn to the last page.

A Taste of New England

Within the vast borders of the U.S.A. travelers have come to know each particular region by the culinary fare it has to offer. The Midwest is synonymous with tender, juicy beef. The South is justifiably proud of its golden fried chicken. And the Southwest receives rave reviews for its spicy enchiladas. Journey with us now to the eastern coast and savor some of the seafood specialties which highlight the many pleasures New England has to offer.

AVOCADO-CRAB DIP

- 1 large avocado, peeled, seeded and cubed
- 1 T. lemon juice
- 1 T. grated onion
- 1 t. Worcestershire sauce
- 1 8-oz. pkg. cream cheese, softened
- ¼ c. sour cream
- ¼ t. salt
- 1 7½-oz. can crab meat, drained, flaked and cartilage removed

In small bowl combine avocado, lemon juice, onion and Worcestershire sauce. Beat until smooth. Add cream cheese, sour cream, and salt; blend. Add crab; refrigerate. Serve with crackers. Serves 8.

SLIMMER CRAB CAKES

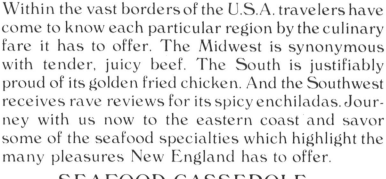

- 1 t. prepared mustard
- 2 T. salad dressing
- 1 egg
- 1 lb. crab meat
  Salt and pepper
- ¼ t. dry mustard
- ½ c. cracker meal
- ¼ c. chopped parsley
  Vegetable oil

Mix prepared mustard, salad dressing and egg together; add crab meat, seasonings, mustard, cracker meal, and parsley. Mix lightly so as not to break up the crab meat. Form into cakes. Fry in small amount of oil until brown; turn and brown on other side. Cakes may also be broiled. Serves 4.

SEAFOOD CASSEROLE

- 1 lb. cooked shrimp
- 4 T. butter
- ½ c. minced onion
- ½ c. minced green pepper
- 1 10½-oz. can cream of mushroom soup
- ¾ c. milk
- 1 2-oz. can chopped mushrooms, with liquid
- 3 c. cooked rice
- 1 6½-oz. can crab meat, drained, flaked, and cartilage removed
- 1 c. buttered bread crumbs
- ½ c. grated Cheddar cheese

Set aside 10 whole shrimp. Cut remaining shrimp in half and set aside. Melt butter in medium-size saucepan and sauté onion and green pepper until tender. Add soup, milk, and mushrooms with liquid; simmer 10 minutes. Fold in rice. Set aside 1½ cups of mixture. To remaining mixture, add cut shrimp and crab meat. Pour in a 2-quart greased casserole. Top with remaining soup mixture; sprinkle with bread crumbs and cheese. Split remaining shrimp lengthwise and arrange on top of casserole. Bake in a 350° oven for 30 minutes. Serves 8.

LOBSTER NEWBURG

- 2 c. cubed, cooked lobster
- ¼ c. butter
- ½ t. salt
  Dash of cayenne
  Dash of nutmeg
- ½ c. cream
- 2 egg yolks, lightly beaten
- 2 T. sherry

Lightly sauté lobster in butter for 3 minutes. Add seasonings and heat 1 minute. Add cream and egg yolks; simmer 3 minutes more. Add sherry and serve in chafing dish. Serves 2 to 4.

Homossassa Jungle In Florida
by Winslow Homer

Florida

I open eyes to mornings crowned with gold
By a sun I've never seen before,
So close to earth it burns, so bright, so bold.
I hear the song of sea that sprays the shore;
I open windows to its siren cry.
And there it is, a world so wide and blue,
With waves and clouds to show where sea meets sky.
I hear palm branches blow with rustling sound,
Like full, starched skirts
That dance and sweep the ground.
I smell the perfume of a thousand flowers
Of blooming plants and shrubs that I can't name.
They glow in clusters, vines and bowers,
Jewel-like in color and wax-like to feel,
So lovely to behold, too perfect to be real.
I walk on white sand beaches in bare feet
And gather washed-up treasures from the deep;
Curved seashells, coral lace, a crab's retreat—
All these, and memories, for me to keep

Annabel Hemley

Paradise

Words, mere words, cannot suffice
To tell the charms of Paradise!
Sky and sea of heavenly blue,
Gay umbrellas tint the view;
Sand and clouds are snowy white—
Whiter for the sun so bright.
Foamy tides lap on the shore.
'Cross the reef you hear a roar!
Look! The surf is dashing high,
Shawls of lace against the sky!

Soon the wind will die away,
Fading with it, surf and spray;
Then upon those sands is rest—
Nature at her loveliest!
Neath the rustling palms, the sea
Bids you "Come and drowse with me.
Lose yourself and dream away;
There's no morrow, just today."

Fred Winslow Rust

Blue Ridge Legacy

Mountains are beautiful
Stretching so high.
Green, leafy branches
Lace-up the sky.
Breezes float gently
On gossamer wings.
Truly God's mountains
Are heavenly things.

Mountains—those lofty
Breathtaking sights.
Fog cloaks their mornings;
Stars gem their nights.
Layer on layer
They come into view,
Ridges of mountains,
Misty and blue.

Mountains are powerful,
Rugged and vast.
Hill, ridge and hollow are
Things that will last.
Standing knee-deep in
The eons of time . . .
Blessed is the child
With mountains to climb!

Alice Leedy Mason

The Land of Evangeline

This is the forest primeval.
The murmuring pines and the hemlocks,
Bearded with moss,
And in garments green,
Indistinct in the twilight,
Stand like Druids of eld,
With voices sad and prophetic,
Stand like harpers hoar,
With beards that rest on their bosoms.
Loud from its rocky caverns,
The deep-voiced neighboring ocean
Speaks and in accents disconsolate
Answers the wail of the forest.

From Evangeline

This is the forest primeval;
But where are the hearts that beneath it
Leaped like the roe,
When he hears in the woodland
The voice of the huntsman?
Where is the thatch-roofed village,
The home of Acadian farmers—
Men whose lives glided on like rivers
That water the woodlands,
Darkened by shadows of earth,
But reflecting an image of heaven?
Waste are those pleasant farms,
And the farmers forever departed!
Scattered like dust and leaves,
When the mighty blasts of October
Seize them, and whirl them aloft,
And sprinkle them far o'er the ocean.
Naught but tradition remains
Of the beautiful village of Grand-Pré.

Ye who believe in affection
That hopes, and endures, and is patient,
Ye who believe in the beauty
And strength of woman's devotion,
List to the mournful tradition,
Still sung by the pines of the forest;
List to a tale of love in Acadie,
Home of the happy.

Henry Wadsworth Longfellow

The Road That Leads to Home

Of all the roads on land or sea
My feet have chanced to roam,
The loveliest of them to me,
Is the road that leads to home.

The road that leads to home, it seems,
Is dearer than the rest,
For it is paved with fondest dreams
Of those I love the best.

It has a friendliness, a cheer,
This road that brings me back
To home and those I love so dear,
That all the others lack.

It is the one road I can wend,
When weary, worn, and spent
And know that waiting at its end,
I shall find peace, content.

Harry E. Brainard

Share
treasured moments with someone you love
in our next issue, Grandparent's *ideals* . . .

- Enjoy a salute to Grandparents in heart-warming prose, poetry, illustrations, and beautiful color photography.

- Feature articles include a journey to Niagara Falls, reminiscences from a fifty-year reunion, and antique trunks as collectors' items.

- Enhance your reading enjoyment or share this delightful keepsake with the special people in your life. A subscription is a thoughtful gift for everyone . . . from children to their parents or grandparents or for a special friend. Fill out either attached card and mail today!

My Old Kentucky Home

Stephen Foster

The sun shines bright on the old Kentucky home,
'Tis summer, the darkies are gay.
The corn-top's ripe and the meadow's in the bloom,
While the birds make music all the day.
The young folks roll on the little cabin floor,
All merry, all happy, and bright.
By 'n' by hard times come a-knocking at the door,
Then, my old Kentucky home, good night!

They hunt no more for the 'possum and the 'coon
On the meadow, the hill, and the shore.
They sing no more by the glimmer of the moon,
On the bench by the old cabin door.
The day goes by like a shadow o'er the heart,
With sorrow where all was delight.
The time has come when the darkies have to part,
Then, my old Kentucky home, good night!

The head must bow and the back will have to bend
Wherever the darky may go.
A few more days and the trouble all will end,
In the fields where the sugarcanes grow,
A few more days for to tote the weary load,
No matter, 'twill never be light,
A few more days till we totter on the road,
Then, my old Kentucky home, good night!

Chorus
Weep no more, my lady,
Oh, weep no more today!
We will sing one song for the old Kentucky home,
For the old Kentucky home, far away.

The beauty and spirit of the Old South are nowhere better recorded than in the lyrics of Stephen Foster, the greatest American composer of the nineteenth century. Best loved are his nostalgic songs and plantation melodies describing life in the Antebellum South. Born in Pennsylvania, Foster never visited the South until he married, yet, his earliest songs reflected a real knowledge of Southern living. Growing up along the Ohio River, young Foster was exposed to the songs and tales of the South by the river traffic to and from New Orleans. He fell in love with the music at a Negro church which he visited with the family's West Indian servant. A strong love for home and family came to be an integral part of his music. His most famous song, "Old Folks at Home," better known as "Way Down upon the Swanee River," was written in 1851. A visit to the Bardstown, Kentucky, home of a relative inspired the writing of his next famous song in 1853. "My Old Kentucky Home," written in the traditional Foster style, created a new era in American folk music. It was adopted as the state song of Kentucky in 1928. The music of America's greatest composer of folk songs, Stephen Foster, was never fully appreciated until years after his death.

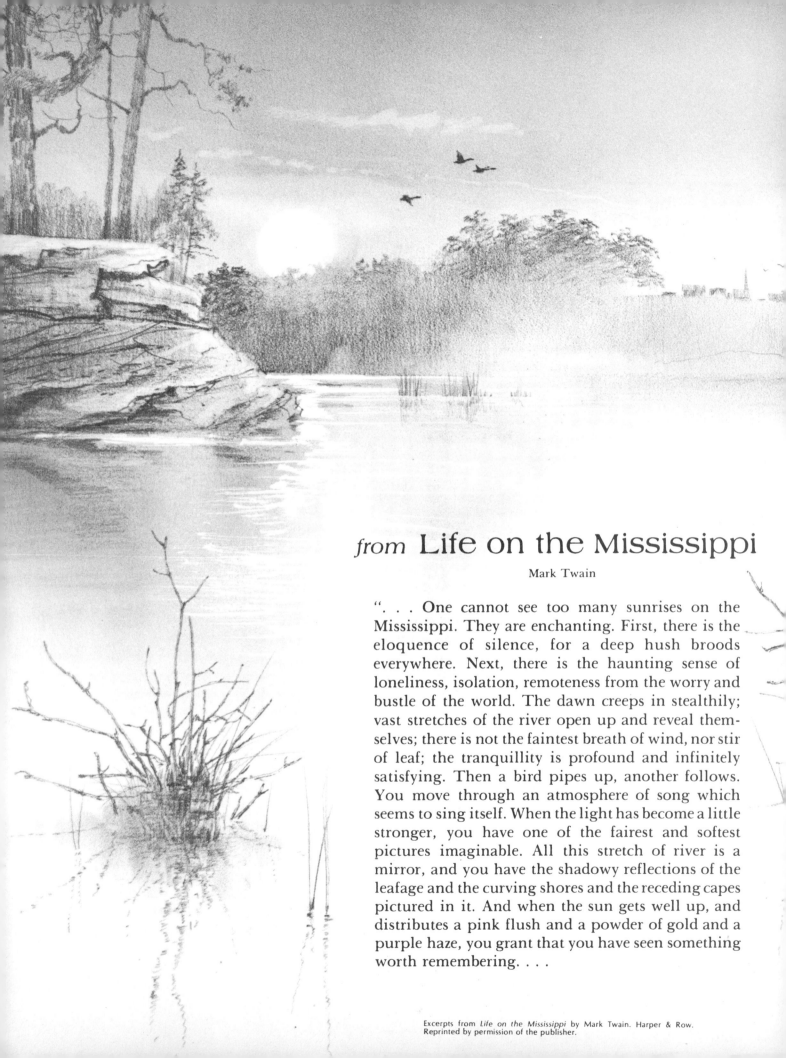

from Life on the Mississippi

Mark Twain

". . . One cannot see too many sunrises on the Mississippi. They are enchanting. First, there is the eloquence of silence, for a deep hush broods everywhere. Next, there is the haunting sense of loneliness, isolation, remoteness from the worry and bustle of the world. The dawn creeps in stealthily; vast stretches of the river open up and reveal themselves; there is not the faintest breath of wind, nor stir of leaf; the tranquillity is profound and infinitely satisfying. Then a bird pipes up, another follows. You move through an atmosphere of song which seems to sing itself. When the light has become a little stronger, you have one of the fairest and softest pictures imaginable. All this stretch of river is a mirror, and you have the shadowy reflections of the leafage and the curving shores and the receding capes pictured in it. And when the sun gets well up, and distributes a pink flush and a powder of gold and a purple haze, you grant that you have seen something worth remembering. . . .

Excerpts from *Life on the Mississippi* by Mark Twain. Harper & Row. Reprinted by permission of the publisher.

. . . The majestic bluffs that overlook the river, along through this region, charm one with the grace and variety of their forms, and the soft beauty of their adornment. The steep, verdant slope, whose base is at the water's edge, is topped by a lofty rampart of broken, turreted rocks, which are exquisitely rich and mellow in color—mainly dark browns and dull greens, but splashed with other tints. And then you have the shining river, winding here and there and yonder, its sweep interrupted at intervals by clusters of wooded islands threaded by silver channels; and you have glimpses of distant villages, asleep upon capes, and of stealthy rafts slipping along in the shade of the forest walls, and of white steamers vanishing around remote points. And it is all as tranquil and reposeful as dreamland, and has nothing this-worldly about it—nothing to hang a fret or a worry upon. . ."

Secrets in Sandstone

The backwater in the gorge is calm, unlike the swift flow of the Wisconsin River's main channel only a few yards beyond the cliff face. But in here, in the dim quiet of the canyon, the tannin colored water forms a still, black pool, broken only by the rolling backs of several huge carp. A tiny stab of sunlight pierces the overhead mantle of ferns and pines atop the cliffs, spotlighting the fish in a rainbow explosion off their shining, wet scales.

Rain coursing down the sides of the sandstone walls has scoured deep grooves along the face of the living stone, as if a playful, giant cat had sharpened its claws after missing a swipe at the fat, lazy fish.

Shadows in the gulch are as deep as the pool, hinting at long-forgotten answers to secrets known only to the cliffs. Cool and dark, even on the hottest summer days, the canyon seems untouched, undisturbed, impervious to the passage of travelers who have explored its recesses for the past hundred years. The rocks, water, damp moss, fish—all ignore that passing and continue on as they have for eons.

The river rolls hungrily along outside, on its 420-mile meandering journey across the face of Wisconsin, from the northern borders with Michigan to its muddy junction with the Mississippi River in the southwestern part of the state. Here in the heart of Wisconsin, the river breaks from the flatlands to twist and turn as would a captured king snake. Five hundred million years ago, the prehistoric seas crashed across this landscape three times, say the geologists, to lay down the thick layers of stone.

Then came the river, long after the oceans had receded. Over the generations—allied with the wind, rain and rock-shattering frost—that water continued its work of wearing away the sandstone, pausing to carve intricate designs in what are now soaring cliffs. For seven and one-fifth miles, the river moves past and through this ageless handiwork.

The resulting formations make up what are known today as the Wisconsin Dells, tourist attractions since the first Indian hunters seven thousand years ago reported their find to neighboring friends. Woodland tribes settled in, creating delicate pottery with designs taken from nature's own. Then, five thousand years ago, came the Mound Builders; though awed by the enormity of the cliffs, they fashioned and molded the land for their own sacred uses.

More tribes followed over the ensuing years: Winnebagoes, Sauk and Chippewas were only the latest in a succession of peoples who appreciated and loved the area they called *Nee-ah-ke-coonah-er-ah*, or "the place where the rocks strike together or nearly strike together."

Even now it is easy to recall the Indian legends about how the land was formed. Imagine the Great Spirit in the form of a huge snake smashing his way southward from his frozen, lakeside home in the north's dense forests. The river swiftly fills the channel dug by the crawling body. The Great Spirit arrives at the rock ridges, part of a spiny range extending toward the Mississippi. He shoves his head through one crevice, then bursts through. His approach frightens off the lesser deities, who are also disguised as snakes.

They flee, their escape routes becoming the canyons leading off from the main chasm. Such is the stuff of dreams.

French-Canadian voyagers in their long, fur-filled freight canoes came hard on the heels of the tribesmen. They used their word *dalles*, meaning trough or narrow passage, to describe this section of the Wisconsin River. From the subsequent slurring of the word and accent change evolved the word *Dells*.

The Dells truly caught the traveler's fancy shortly after the Civil War when former lumberman and river pilot Leroy Gates announced that he had purchased a pleasure boat. Gates said the vessel could be used for exploring the "numerous occult caves of the district." His pitch went on to promise that "depressed spirits can be alleviated, gloom and melancholy soon dispelled and the mind greatly invigorated" by a riverboat tour.

At the same time, stereoscopic slides of the Dells taken by noted photographer H.H. Bennett became more popular. As the fame of these natural wonders spread across the country, tourists began flocking to central Wisconsin.

Ever since, the Dells have been among the most popular attractions in the Midwest. While commercial developments have sprung up in the small communities near the river, the Wisconsin remains all-powerful—still carving, chipping and creating.

The Upper Dells, north of a huge dam in the city of Wisconsin Dells, are home for numerous fanciful formations named over the years by passersby: Swallow's Nest, High Rock, Romance Cliff, Black Hawk's Head, Giant's Shield, Alligator's Head and others. Almost every outcropping has a tag. Cold Water Canyon, Witches' Gulch and Stand Rock lead off from the main river and are showcases for the tour guides. On the Lower Dells, below the dam, are the Witches' Window, the Football, Grand Piano, the Rocky Islands, Ink Stand and similar geographic delights—their names indicating their shapes.

The seasons bring lovely, everchanging intricacies to the Dells. Spring urges the delicate wild flowers to carpet the clifftops. Summer paints a heavy olivine across the land, with only the white birches in bas-relief. Autumn dances across the woods, making the world shimmer in a thousand hues. Winter's harshness hardens the river's surface, but never its vibrant soul.

The Dells are constant and steady, always delightful. In the soft ever-evening shadows of the canyons, while the fish play tag with the sun streams, the secrets of this land may be revealed. But the visitor must listen, watch and, most importantly, dream a bit.

Martin Hintz

"Back Roads" Beauty

Bea Bourgeois

One of our national tendencies seems to be an obsession with speed. Particularly when we travel by car, "What time did you leave?" becomes a question of the utmost importance. It is almost a point of honor to shave fifteen or twenty minutes off the established driving time between, for example, Milwaukee and northern Wisconsin.

Freeways—those monotonous, hypnotic stretches of pale concrete—have one advantage: they take the traveler from Point A to Point B in the shortest possible amount of time. But we've discovered that speed isn't everything.

A few years ago we invested in a set of County Maps of Wisconsin, available from the Department of Transportation for $3.50 plus tax. The 72 maps are alphabetically arranged, so it's easy to plot a trip up and down or across the state. My husband put the maps in a sturdy three-ring binder, and we keep the book under the front seat of the car.

That book has become a magical "Open Sesame" for our family. We have abandoned the popular I-94 route for our trips to Hayward, and instead we use Wisconsin's state and county roads. We may not break any speed records, but we've discovered some wonderful things about Wisconsin and the people who live here.

Of course, we have been occasionally stuck behind a tractor or a milk truck for a few miles, but so what? We've had a chance to see endless acres of sunflowers being raised for seed; huge fields of potatoes near Stevens Point; a beautiful stray deer poised hesitantly at the edge of a woods; mink and turkey farms, some with spooky, old, abandoned buildings; real, working farmers plowing and threshing their land—rare sights for city dwellers.

When we left Milwaukee at Eastertime one year, we drove as far as Princeton, in Green Lake County, and stopped for breakfast. Purely by chance we discovered a bright and cheery "Ma and Pa" cafe where several local residents were trading jokes over their morning coffee.

Our meal was scrumptious: freshly fried eggs, hot buttered toast, crisp pork sausage, and French toast sizzling from the griddle. Coffee cups were refilled regularly, always with a smile and a friendly remark. It was a pleasure to eat food that had not been precooked and prepackaged.

About an hour out of Princeton our youngest son discovered that he had left a favorite cap in the restaurant. On the way back to Milwaukee, after nearly a week had passed, we stopped at the cafe and were stunned when the smiling, grandmotherly cook handed David his cap. "I saved it for you," she explained with a grin. I'm not sure, but somehow I don't think that would have happened at an ultra modern, fast-food franchise restaurant!

We passed through thirteen different Wisconsin counties on that trip. In tiny towns, we stopped at grocery stores for treats of all kinds; we bought fresh eggs along the way; we marveled at the sea of red cranberries in storage tanks near Wisconsin Rapids, where the road cuts right between the bogs.

We stretched our legs in small rural cemeteries and were awed by the antiquity of some of the grave markers. We were able to show our sons what wild asparagus looks like, and we stopped at a farm to buy a bag of straw that made a comfortable bed for the Infant in the Christmas creche months later.

After driving through paper mill country near Nekoosa and Port Edwards, we went west on highway 73 into Clark County where we discovered a lovely County Park outside of Greenwood. We had packed a picnic lunch and were blessed with a sunny, mild day; it was a refreshing pause to munch our sandwiches in the park with a gentle, flowing river for a backdrop. The boys worked off some excess energy throwing sticks into the river and Frisbees at one another.

We have happened onto county fairs and small town anniversary celebrations, and been overwhelmed with local hospitality. We have meandered through intriguing antique shops in out-of-the-way places. We have enjoyed some of Wisconsin's lovely spring wildflowers—marsh marigolds, violets, trilliums, buttercups, and Indian paint brushes.

Farm youngsters have waved to the toot of our horn from their perches high on a tractor or a hay wagon. Their parents have shared a luscious raspberry harvest with us—for significantly less than we would have paid at the supermarket. Old advertising signs on barns and fence posts have brought back memories of gentler times when speed didn't matter at all.

Traveling the state and county highways has given us an unbeatable opportunity to learn more about Wisconsin and to appreciate its people. Our family is convinced that superhighways are efficient, fast, and boring. We don't mind a raised eyebrow or two when we answer the inevitable "How long did it take you?" There are a lot of advantages to being slow pokes!

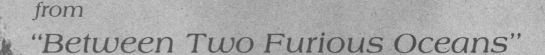

from
"Between Two Furious Oceans"

You are the quiet bays and the lonely shadows of the firs;
The vast green acres blanketing the wide Alberni hills,
Hemlock and cedar and spruce . . . proud with everlasting green;
Cold blue glaciers, spilling their life into roaring Atlin creeks;

Meadows in the clouds and valleys mute with solitude . . .
You are the heaving lakes, the rolling, green-jacketed hills
Of Stormont and Dundas; roaring Niagara and the swift
Cold current of the Ottawa, hedged with silver birch . . .

You are the dainty meadows and the lazy, dappled streams
Of Joliette; the cool, sweet whisper of Laurentian breezes;
The river willows and the gracious elms; chipmunk and beaver
And the antlered deer; the green, windswept curve of Gaspé loin . . .

You are the caravans that spanned the plains and the axe that hewed
The cedars for Camosun's Fort; you are the arm that fought
The torrent through Kicking Horse, paddling to the ocean from the heights . . .

You are a new nation, the raw nugget;
The untempered blade, the uncontrolled flame . . .
You are the white-hot steel, taking your shape
Under the hammerblows of Time. . . .

Dick Diespecker

In a little while all interest was taken up in stretching our necks and watching for the pony-rider—the fleet messenger who sped across the continent from St. Joe to Sacramento, carrying letters nineteen hundred miles in eight days!

The Pony Express

Samuel Clemens

Think of that for perishable horse and human flesh and blood to do! The pony-rider was usually a little bit of a man, brimful of spirit and endurance. No matter what time of the day or night his watch came on, and no matter whether it was winter or summer, raining, snowing, hailing, or sleeting, or whether his beat was a level, straight road or a crazy trail over mountain crags and precipices, or whether it led through peaceful regions or regions that swarmed with hostile Indians, he must be always ready to leap into the saddle and be off like the wind! There was no idling-time for a pony-rider on duty. He rode fifty miles without stopping, by daylight, moonlight, starlight, or through the blackness of darkness—just as it happened. He rode a splendid horse that was born for a racer and fed and lodged like a gentleman, kept him at his utmost speed for ten miles, and then, as he came crashing up to the station where stood two men holding fast a fresh, impatient steed, the transfer of rider and mailbag was made in the twinkling of an eye, and away flew the eager pair and were out of sight before the spectator could get hardly the ghost of a look. Both rider and horse went flying light. The rider's dress was thin, and fitted close; he wore a roundabout, and a skullcap, and tucked his pantaloons into his boot tops like a race-rider. He carried no arms—he carried nothing that was not absolutely necessary, for even the postage of his literary freight was worth five dollars a letter. He got but little frivolous correspondence to carry—his bag had business letters in it, mostly. His horse was stripped of all unnecessary weight, too. He wore a little wafer of a racing-saddle, and no visible blanket. He wore light shoes, or none at all. The little flat mail pockets strapped under the rider's thighs would each hold about the bulk of a child's primer. They held many and many an important business chapter and newspaper letter, but these were written on paper as airy and thin as gold-leaf, nearly, and thus bulk and weight were economized. The stagecoach traveled about a hundred to a hundred and twenty-five miles a day (twenty-four hours), the pony-rider about two hundred and fifty. There were about eighty pony-riders in the saddle all the time, night and day, stretching in a long, scattering procession from Missouri to California, forty flying eastward, and forty toward the west, and among them making four hundred gallant horses earn a stirring livelihood and see a deal of scenery every single day.

We had a consuming desire, from the beginning, to see a pony-rider, but somehow or other all that passed us and all that met us managed to streak by in the night, and so we heard only a whiz and a hail, and the swift phantom of the desert was gone before we could get our heads out of the windows. But now we were expecting one along every moment and would see him in broad daylight. Presently the driver exclaims:

"Here he comes!"

Every neck is stretched further, and every eye strained wider. Away across the endless dead level of the prairie a black speck appears against the sky, and it is plain that it moves. Well, I should think so! In a second or two it becomes a horse and rider, rising and falling, rising and falling—sweeping toward us nearer and nearer—growing more and more distinct, more and more sharply defined— nearer and still nearer, and the flutter of the hoofs comes faintly to the ear—another instant a whoop and a hurrah from our upper deck, a wave of the rider's hand, but no reply, and man and horse burst past our excited faces, and go swinging away like a belated fragment of a storm!

So sudden is it all, and so like a flash of unreal fancy, that but for the flake of white foam left quivering and perishing on a mail-sack after the vision had flashed by and disappeared, we might have doubted whether we had seen any actual horse and man at all, maybe.

We rattled through Scott's Bluffs Pass, by and by. It was along here somewhere that we first came across genuine and unmistakable alkali water in the road, and we cordially hailed it as a first-class curiosity, and a thing to be mentioned with éclat in letters to the ignorant at home. This water gave the road a soapy appearance, and in many places the ground looked as if it had been whitewashed. I think the strange alkali water excited us as much as any wonder we had come upon yet, and I know we felt very complacent and conceited, and better satisfied with life after we had added it to our list of things which we had seen and some other people had not.

We crossed the sandhills near the scene of the Indian mail robbery and massacre of 1856, wherein the driver and conductor perished, and also all the passengers but one, it was supposed; but this must have been a mistake, for at different times afterward on the Pacific coast I was personally acquainted with a hundred and thirty-three or four people who were wounded during that massacre, and barely escaped with their lives. There was no doubt of the truth of it—I had it from their own lips. One of these parties told me that he kept coming across arrowheads in his system for nearly seven years after the massacre; and another of them told me that he was stuck so literally full of arrows that after the Indians were gone and he could raise up and examine himself, he could not restrain his tears, for his clothes were completely ruined.

The most trustworthy tradition avers, however, that only one man, a person named Babbitt, survived the massacre, and he was desperately wounded. He dragged himself on his hands and knee (for one leg was broken) to a station several miles away. He did it during portions of two nights, lying concealed one day and part of another, and for more than forty hours suffering unimaginable anguish from hunger, thirst, and bodily pain. The Indians robbed the coach of everything it contained, including quite an amount of treasure.

Paha-Sapa: Sacred Land of the Spirits

To the goldseekers they were giant treasure troves in which lay hidden the keys to men's fortunes. To weary pioneers traveling west they were a forest oasis, a relief from the bleached, barren wasteland of *mako sica*—the bad land. To the ten tribes of the Sioux nation they were the center of the world, the sacred land of the spirits, the place to commune with *Wakan Tanka*—the Great Spirit. The Indians called them *Paha-Sapa*—the Black Hills.

Certainly "Black Hills" is no misnomer; from a distance they do appear black, rising out of the flat, colorless grasslands of South Dakota. But at closer range the deep green of ponderosa pine forest, spreading across 5,000 square miles, stands out against the clear, blue sky of the plains. Unlike the adolescent Rockies, these ancient mountains do not severely affect the weather patterns and, therefore, do not experience the inevitable daily drenchings common in the higher ranges. Fair weather and blue skies generally prevail, providing a comfortable atmosphere in which visitors can explore the many swiftly-flowing streams, glassy-surfaced lakes and natural as well as man-made landmarks scattered throughout this region.

Only an hour's drive east of the Black Hills the lunar-like landscape of Badlands National Monument thrusts its saw-tooth peaks above the surrounding prairie. Any trip to the Black Hills would be incomplete without a visit to this landmark. In Rapid City, the eastern gateway to the Hills, the School of Mines displays an exhibit of extinct animals that once roamed the lush swamps of the presently arid Badlands. These animals include not only the camels, saber-toothed cats, fox-sized horses and pig-shaped oreodonts of geologically recent time, but also the alligators, snail-like ammonites and giant sea turtles of prehistory.

As these fossilized life forms testify, the Badlands originated as the floor of a shallow inland sea. After the same forces that elevated the Rocky Mountains lifted and drained this floor, small streams cut rolling hills and broad valleys. Raging rivers later stormed down from the mountains with much rocky debris, leveling the former sea bottom into a vast floodplain. As the subsequent marshes evaporated into the present grasslands, nature's eroding forces carved out of this mountain sediment the fantastic shapes of the Badlands.

Such forces continue to strip away these deceptive mountains, laying bare the source of their descriptive and highly appropriate name. Although they have the appearance of solid rock, the mud- and siltstone Badlands do not have the substance of rock to combat the rains and melting snows constantly and rapidly dissolving their fragile crust. Underneath this dry, protective crust, the soil is sodden, slippery and, as a result, very difficult to traverse. Without the modern-day convenience of established paths, the early trailblazers—Indians and French Canadian trappers—found the terrain nearly impossible to cross; hence the name "Badlands."

Today, the Badlands are more easily accessible via reinforced trails and a paved road. At the heart of the monument, Cedar Pass provides a museum, campground and visitor center, which offers daytime nature hikes and nighttime amphitheater programs. Without disturbing the natural environment, these conveniences keep within reach the wild and transient beauty of the Badlands.

Several miles to the west, however, a more permanent landmark, this one man-made, promises to endure through the ages both physically and spiritually.

Over half a century ago, the peaceful serenity of the Black Hills was shattered by drilling jackhammers and exploding dynamite. Sculptor Gutzon Borglum had begun his most difficult yet intriguing challenge: to carve on the exposed face of a towering granite bluff America's shrine to democracy—Mount Rushmore National Memorial. Fourteen years later, and with no finer tools than these ordinarily destructive forces, Borglum had created a masterpiece of artistry and engineering dedicated to the principles, dreams and aspirations of an entire nation.

Originally conceived by state historian Doane Robinson as a tribute to the heroic figures of the west, the project took on a more significant dimension when he approached well-known artist, Gutzon Borglum with his plan. The idealistic artist believed that the mountain should stand not only for the west, but for the whole country as well. He was convinced that no one could better personify those qualities responsible for America's perpetuation than the Presidents of the United States. For that reason, and for their outstanding examples of leadership, Borglum selected George Washington, Thomas Jefferson, Theodore Roosevelt and Abraham Lincoln for his mountain monument.

In 1927, Borglum and his trained crew dangled over the edge of the 6,000-foot cliff in bosuns' chairs, and began chipping away at the granite wall. From small-scale plaster models they fashioned granite heads sixty feet in height. Although they intended to carve the figures complete to the waist, the heads alone eventually required nearly fourteen years to finish.

They encountered many delays caused by the rock's stubborness. The biggest setback occurred when it became obvious that the granite would not conform to the contours of the first face. Forced to abandon this first attempt, Borglum had to blast it off the mountain. But these delays were never a waste of time, only valuable learning experiences essential in preventing future delays.

Finally, after battling through almost half a million tons of tough, unyielding rock, the aging artist/engineer saw his sculpture nearing completion. In 1941, at the age of seventy-four, Gutzon Borglum died, leaving a lasting tribute to America in the land of *Paha-Sapa*.

The Black Hills are still the sacred land of the spirits, especially the spirit of America.

Rachel Knight

There's a church in the valley by the wildwood,
No lovelier spot in the dale;
No place is so dear to my childhood
As the little brown church in the vale.

Oh, come to the church in the wildwood,
To the trees where the wild flowers bloom;
Where the parting hymn will be chanted,
We will weep by the side of the tomb.

From the church in the valley by the wildwood,
When day fades away into night,
I would fain from this spot of my childhood
Wing my way to the mansions of light.

Oh, come, come, come, come,
Come to the church in the wildwood;
Oh, come to the church in the vale;
No spot is so dear to my childhood
As the little brown church in the vale.

William S. Pitts

The Little Brown Church in the Vale

On many a Sunday morning in church, people have sung the uplifting words, "Come to the church in the wildwood; come to the church in the vale." The romantic birth of this song, "The Church in the Wildwood," is linked to another equally inspiring story—that of the coincidental building of an actual church which came to be known as "The Little Brown Church in the Vale."

The story began in 1857, when a young music teacher, William S. Pitts, traveling by stagecoach from his home in southern Wisconsin to visit his bride-to-be in Fredericksburg, Iowa, stopped for a rest at noon in the little pioneer town of Bradford, Iowa. As the young, enamored Pitts strolled through town, he came to a spot of rare and tranquil beauty. He was deeply touched by the loveliness and serenity of the scene, and visualized a small, rural church set amidst the rolling green hills, lush foliage and ancient trees. When Pitts returned home, his thoughts drifted back to the image of a country church in the midst of that pastoral setting. The young music teacher sat down and wrote the song, "The Little Brown Church in the Vale," then put the composition away in a desk drawer where it remained gathering dust.

When Pitts returned to Bradford years later, he was stunned by what he saw. In the six years that had passed, the people of Bradford had decided to build a church right in the very spot where Pitts had imagined one. The project was begun in 1859 when Rev. John K. Nutting came to Bradford to serve as pastor. At that time, the people were worshipping in a log cabin, a lawyer's office, a hotel dining room, a school house and an abandoned store without doors or windows. The members of the church were few in number and poor, but they were inspired by the young pastor to try to build a church. The struggling congregation of pioneers contributed most of the logs, lumber, and stones and much of the work to finish the building. The bell in the tower was donated by a couple in New York, and its coming was such a wondrous event that it was rung constantly during its trip from Dubuque to Bradford.

On dedication day in 1864, Mr. Pitts' voice class sang his song about the "little brown church" in public for the first time. Soon afterwards, Pitts took the song to Chicago, where it was published. He used the money he earned from its publication to help finance his schooling for a medical degree, then returned with his wife to Fredericksburg, where he set up practice. The song quickly won local recognition, but little did its author know that one day it would capture the hearts and minds of people across the land and around the world.

At the turn of the century, the church became inactive for a time when the community of Bradford all but disappeared after the town failed to acquire a railroad. However, a railroad did come to the nearby town of Nashua, which steadily grew as the town of Bradford declined. For a time, the church building was closed, and weeds grew high across the unkept grounds. Its brown paint soon lost its luster, but the stouthearted little congregation kept faith in someday witnessing the church's revival. They could never have foreseen the future fame of their little "church in the vale."

In 1910, a group of vocalists from Iowa known as the "Weatherwax Brothers Male Quartet," who were gaining in popularity, performing at chautauquas and social gatherings around the country and Canada, introduced the song into their programs. With each singing they would tell the story of how Dr. Pitts wrote the song and the location of the real church in the wildwood. Out of a repertoire of more than three hundred numbers, "The Church in the Wildwood," as it was later renamed, was the one song America remembered.

Today, situated in the little northeast Iowa town of Nashua, the church continues to grow. Many thousands of visitors each year have journeyed to "the little brown church." Some have come for the sacrament of baptism, some to take vows of matrimony, and others, simply to experience the same peace, comfort and joy that a young music teacher felt and recorded in a prophetic song more than a hundred years ago.

Michele Arrieh

Arizona

Come with me to Arizona,
a copper land of flowing mountains
brown with age,
rainbow gorges, desert sand and purple sage
where a thousand miles of sunset throw
a fading glow
into a star-filled night.

Then when morning rises, take my hand
and linger
in this golden land with me
where barefoot boys and barefoot girls
stayed and built adobe dreams.

Listen!
Happy laughter fills the spaces.
Sturdy cacti
bare their faces to the blistering sun.
Farther on,
away from dust, lie emerald valleys.

Follow me
and I will show you hidden trails,
mountain pastures,
crystal water cold as ice
with fish,
and air with spice of cedar tree and pine
where deer and squirrel live
in primal paradise.

Almyra Noller

Four Corners: Gateway to the Southwest

Beverly Wiersum Charette

Travelers following U.S. 160 spot the sign indicating "Point of interest ahead" and pull off the highway. Forcing themselves out of their air-conditioned, 72-degree cars into the sun-conditioned, 100-degree desert, they glance around expectantly, hoping to marvel at another of nature's remarkably artistic accomplishments peculiar to this area. Instead, they are greeted by a lonely, man-made marker set in stone labeled "Four Corners"—the only point in the United States common to four states. In the midst of a remote and desolate desert, the cornerstone of America's southwest struggles to remain above the sand.

Initially, this point of interest, shared by Colorado, New Mexico, Arizona and Utah, leaves visitors with an impression far from interesting; in all four directions the eyes meet nothing but sun, sand and sagebrush. The marker itself seems ludicrous, relying on imaginary man-made boundaries as a meaning for existence. But upon more thoughtful inspection, the seasoned traveler, no stranger to the artistry of erosion commonplace in this part of the country, appreciates the marker's simplicity as it stands sentinel over the unique scenic beauty typical of the southwest.

Slender arches of burnt ocher defy gravity, spanning incredible distances with no other support than the air. Large, odd-shaped boulders balance precariously on pinpoint supports, threatening to topple at any moment. Others cling stubbornly to a smooth, sloping rock surface like crumbs to a cookie sheet. The mouth of a stone monkey's head is frozen in mid-chatter. In this delusory state of suspended animation the only movement is the subtle stirring of the wind—the heartbeat of the southwest—lightly fingering the sandstone formations of Arches National Park.

In reality, these stone sculptures are undergoing a continuous process of decay caused by nature's eroding forces. This greatest concentration of natural arches in the world began forming long ago when the earth bulged out of its seams and cracked an entire layer of sandstone. Rain, frost and thaw, and other weathering agents widened these cracks until they cut through a narrow wall, or "fin," to form a hole. Subsequent rockfalls enlarged the hole, creating an arch. Eventually all the graceful arches of the southwest, including the eighty-eight discovered within the boundaries of this park, will collapse, leaving only their end buttresses to jut out into the desert sun.

But the arches have many years left before crumbling into oblivion. Visitors can still experience nature's artistry in the land of eternal sunset.

An overly ambitious maid, the mighty southwestern wind sweeps up from the direction of Four Corners and attacks the unanchored silt and sand of the San Luis Valley in south central Colorado. Vacuuming up this debris, dragged down from the mountains by rivers and streams, the wind carries it across the flat, open plain to the foot of the Sangre de Cristo range. Here, the nearly impenetrable horseshoe barrier formed by the mountains forces the wind to surrender its heavy burden before whistling through the gaps and openings in the range. Raining sand, the wind shapes a miniature western Sahara—Great Sand Dunes National Monument.

These mountainous dunes represent centuries of the slow yet constant eastward progression of sand in the San Luis River Valley. The sand dunes originate by accumulating around some object, usually a rare sample of hardy plant life. As the wind continues to deposit sand, shifting it from windward to leeward, the dunes begin to advance toward the mountains. En route, they engulf anything that crosses their path, often leaving skeletons of trees in their wake.

Though dwarfed by the nearby mountains, including some of the highest peaks in the continental divide, the Great Sand Dunes are the tallest dunes in the United States, some towering over 700 feet. Against the shadowy, jagged peaks of the southern Rockies, the dunes stand out in brilliant, smooth contrast.

Jagged shafts of brilliant white light pierce billowing, black clouds. Enraged by such treatment, the clouds rumble a protest amplified by the depths of a massive chasm. Then, dragging the unsheltered earth into this meteorological battle, they pound the dusty soil with steely torrents. Just when the storm threatens to continue indefinitely, however, the sky steps in as moderator and splits the clouds, emitting radiant sunshine to bathe the stratified canyon walls with a soft, buttery glow. It is small wonder that out of such an event, American composer Ferde Grofé created his *Grand Canyon Suite*.

Often referred to as the eighth wonder of the world, northern Arizona's Grand Canyon of the Colorado has, with good reason, stimulated much creative expression. In beauty and magnitude it cannot be equaled. As a living record of time it stands alone. Written upon its walls are the history and prehistory of the southwest, dating back two billion years. The Colorado River, a meticulous archeologist, persistently excavates the canyon, revealing past seabeds, estuaries, sand dunes, deserts and river deltas, which contain the story of life on earth. That story continues today as new varieties of common plant and animal species, such as the pink Grand Canyon rattlesnake, evolve by adapting to the unique conditions of canyon life.

Whether standing on the mile-deep canyon floor or teetering on the edge of the North Rim, no visitor can escape the immediate and overwhelming power of the Grand Canyon.

As the Guadalupe Mountains consume the liquid, desert sun, an intense stillness pervades the atmosphere, overwhelming the uninvited intruders. Then, barely perceptible, the silence of moving air emanates from the depths of the yawning hole opposite the audience. Building to a crescendo, this silence explodes into a flutter of swirling wings; the night sky over Carlsbad Caverns National Park, New Mexico, is alive with the 300,000 residents of Bat Cave.

Unquestionably a remarkable spectacle, this nightly exodus was what originally lured the first white men to investigate the deceivingly empty land along New Mexico's southern border. Searching for the point of origin of this great black horde's nocturnal raid on insects, they discovered not only Bat Cave, but also the ground-level entrance cave leading to an enormous subterranean system of corridors and chambers. More than 800 feet directly beneath the desert floor, the interior of nature's netherworld palace lay hidden.

Today, visitors can reach the caverns either by braving a steep, switchback trail, or riding a high-speed elevator. Once inside the fourteen-acre Big Room, the main cavern with a ceiling soaring to 285 feet, they are free to explore the seven miles of caverns open to them. Subtle illumination reveals still, green pools and inverted stone icicles, more accurately referred to as stalagmites, as well as their counterparts, stalactites. In the constant 56-degree dampness, winter or summer, visitors can view these stone sculptures deposited by the slow, interminable seepage of water begun thousands of years ago and continuing today.

Temples of the Lord

How thrilled, we stand beneath the peaks
  That tower up to God
And gaze upon their ragged cliffs,
  Where man has never trod!

Majestic mountains, lofty, bold,
  Projecting in the sky,
Seem mighty temples of the Lord,
  With spires of crags on high.

And all His creatures of the woods,
  The birds that chirp and sing,
The roaming deer, the lizards small,
  Each day are worshiping.

And we, who wander in their midst,
  And up the steep trails climb,
Are moved to cherish only thoughts
  Which are the most sublime.

The wilds of nature kindle strong,
  In most of us, the best.
Their tranquil silence brings a peace,
  Their changing shadows, rest.

And like the psalmist, we look up
  Unto the hills for strength;
Unto the heights, whence cometh help
  For all our needs, at length.

Agnes Davenport Bond

The Eagle

James Gates Percival

Bird of the broad and sweeping wing,
　Thy home is high in heaven,
Where the wide storms their banners fling,
　And the tempest-clouds are driven.
Thy throne is on the mountaintop;
　Thy fields, the boundless air;
And hoary peaks, that proudly prop
　The skies, thy dwellings are.

Thou art perched aloft, on the beetling crag,
　And the waves are white below,
And on, with a haste that cannot lag,
　They rush in an endless flow.
Again thou hast plumed thy wing for flight,
　To lands beyond the sea,
And away, like a spirit wreathed in light,
　Thou hurriest, wild and free.

Lord of the boundless realm of air
　In thy imperial name
The hearts of the bold and ardent dare
　The dangerous path of fame.
Beneath the shade of thy golden wings
　The Roman legions bore,
From the river of Egypt's cloudy springs,
　Their pride to the polar shore.

For thee they fought, for thee they fell,
　And their oath on thee was laid;
To thee the clarions raised their swell,
　And the dying warrior prayed.
Thou wert, through an age of death and fears,
　The image of pride and power,
Till the gathered rage of a thousand years
　Burst forth in one awful hour.

And then, a deluge of wrath it came,
　And the nations shook with dread;
And it swept the earth, till its fields were flame,
　And piled with the mingled dead.
Kings were rolled in the wasteful flood,
　With the low and crouching slave;
And together lay in a shroud of blood,
　The coward and the brave.

And where was then thy fearless flight?
　O'er the dark and mysterious sea,
To the land that caught the setting light,
　The cradle of liberty.

There, on the silent and lonely shore,
　For ages I watched alone,
And the world, in its darkness, asked no more
　Where the glorious bird had flown.

But then, came a bold and hardy few,
　And they breasted the unknown wave;
I saw from far the wandering crew,
　And I knew they were high and brave.
I wheeled around the welcome bark,
　As it sought the desolate shore,
And up to heaven, like a joyous lark,
　My quivering pinions bore.

And now, that bold and hardy few
　Are a nation wide and strong;
And danger and doubt I have led them through,
　And they worship me in song;
And over their bright and glancing arms,
　On field, and lake, and sea,
With an eye that fires, and a spell that charms,
　I guide them to victory!

Crater Lake

Crater Lake, relic of an ancient volcanic explosion, is rimmed by fifteen miles of sheer cliffs two thousand feet high and as jagged in outline as the edges of a broken bottle. Nearly round and more than five miles across, the lake is more than a mile above sea level on the crest of the Cascade Range in Oregon—an expanse of water so still and so remarkably pure that it looks as deep and clean and blue as the stratosphere. An eerie stillness seems to trap and intensify the mountain silence. Strangely, after a short time one's ears begin to ring as if deafened by reverberations of the cataclysm which consumed a mountaintop.

But what captures the imagination is the specter of that vanished mountain, for it is impossible to admire the lake without reconstructing the phenomenon which created it. While Crater Lake plays tricks with the ears and its diamond brilliance is a feast for the eyes, the mind is busy recreating an event which took place about six thousand years ago.

The geology of the spectacular cliffs surrounding Crater Lake provides clues to the structure of the twelve-thousand-foot-high peak known as Mount Mazama, the name conferred on the area by local Indians long after the mountain was destroyed. Its complex and roughly conical shape was brought into being over hundreds of thousands of years by successive lava flows from the volcano. These layers can still be seen as clearly as the age rings of a log. Entire sections of cliff comprise funnel-shaped masses of lava showing where the side vents opened in the mature mountain, oozing molten rock down the slopes and indicating that the mountain did not have the geometric outlines of nearby Mount St. Helens and Mount Hood. Harder materials, forced from below into cracks in the mountainside, remain now as buttresses, jutting out sharply and in a variety of colors. These variegations, vents and buttresses give a clear idea of the shape and size of Mount Mazama.

The U-shaped dips in the skyline around Crater Lake show where the side of the mountain was scoured into deep valleys and gorges by glaciers. Scratches in the glacier-polished rocks show the extent and direction of glaciers during successive ice ages. When the explosion occurred, the glaciers were in their last period of retreat. The events which reduced the mountain to rubble took place within only a matter of days.

The tribes of Indians inhabiting the forests and tundra of the Northwest must have stood in awe and fear as the great clouds of white-hot ash boiled miles high from the top of the mountain. Carried by the wind, it melted glaciers and set forests alight where it fell, covering five thousand square miles to a depth of up to twenty feet. Dust covered the landscape for six hundred miles to the north, far into present-day British Columbia. In modern times, only the destruc-tion of Krakatoa in the East Indies, in 1883, bears comparison, and that was heard three thousand miles away. The Mount Mazama explosion would probably have been heard as far away as Hawaii, Lake Erie and the Gulf Coast.

So much material, over half its height, was blasted from the mountain that the reservoir deep inside could not replenish itself in time to prevent the creation of a vast cavern. Almost eight cubic miles of solid rock shattered into fragments and slid with a crescendo of noise and rising dust into the hole beneath.

When the dust settled, a four-thousand-foot-deep caldera had formed in place of a mile-high peak. The rain and melting snow half-filled the crater to the point where evaporation and seepage balanced precipitation. Later, a minor eruption formed Wizard Island, a small cone of cinders in the lake. The lake maintains a constant depth of 1,932 feet, making it one of the deepest lakes in the world. Some algae at the lake bottom are the only natural life there. Rainbow trout and kokanee salmon were recently introduced into the lake, but the water proved too pure for them.

Geologically, the great Mount Mazama volcano is now extinct, its energy expended. Crater Lake remains, beautiful and silent. During most of the year the craggy terrain around the lake is covered by deep drifts of snow, the dazzling white enriching the vivid blue of the water. The reflection, blurred here and there by soft breezes, seems unreal, and the imagination is easily stirred to a vivid recreation of the holocaust that consumed a mountain.

John Dyson

Fallen leaves do not rustle underfoot; they crumple like wet paper. Broken branches bend or tear, but do not snap. Soggy twigs fold rather than crack. It is a wonderland where delicate ferns and mosses flourish in the shade of some of the world's mightiest trees—an enchanting, mysterious and magical wilderness that is quite unlike any other place on earth.

The Olympic rain forest covers three deep, glacier-formed valleys on the western slopes of the Olympic Mountains, near the coast of Washington. Technically, a rain forest is an area that receives more than eighty inches of rain annually. Here the moisture-laden Pacific Ocean airstreams are deflected upward so sharply by the mountains that they are condensed by the cold air to form an astonishing yearly average of 142 inches of rain.

Olympic Rain Forest

The characteristic of a true rain forest is perpetual dampness. The sodden, still atmosphere creates a natural greenhouse, where ferns, mosses and lichens cover every twig, branch and stump. Clubmosses trail from branches in long, wispy beards. Velvety mosses quilt the rough bark of tall conifers and shroud the pulpy fibers of rotting logs. Ferns form crowns high up in the trees and tiny toadstools grow in the dark, damp hollows of tree stumps.

It is more like an underwater world than a forest. Short flashes of sunlight break through the green canopy of trees like reflections on the sea, while the light at ground level is a dim aquarium-green. The feathery mosses resemble wafting seaweed, and the impression of being underwater is heightened by the sensation of weightlessness one has when walking on the thick-sprung mattress of spongy mosses, ferns and creepers.

The Olympic rain forest is unique, not only in its atmosphere but also as a phenomenon of nature. It is the world's only true coniferous rain forest and the only temperate rain forest. Unlike all other rain forests, which are found in the tropics, it is not a dense tangle of vines and creepers because browsing black-tailed deer and Roosevelt elk keep the under-growth under control. Consequently, the forest is a delight to walk through, and wildlife abounds. Tiny Douglas squirrels and snowshoe hares scurry about, cougars and coyotes stalk their prey, beavers feed on the bark of alders along the banks of dashing rivers, and black bears fish for salmon and steelhead trout. The distant hammering of a woodpecker or the cackling of a jay emphasizes the stillness, and there is always the steady, muffled rustle of water dripping down from leaf to leaf, even when it is not actually raining.

Bastions of the forest are its great trees, which average two hundred and fifty feet in height, some topping three hundred feet. The largest known specimens of four species—western hemlock, Douglas fir, red alder and western red cedar—are found in or near its borders. Strangely, their roots go down only three or four feet, so eventually the giants are toppled by the winter gales, often gusting to more than one hundred miles an hour, that funnel up the forest valleys.

After a tree falls, the process of decay begins. This decay is a particularly potent force on which the renewal of the rain forest depends. Within five years the fallen tree is covered by a dense mat of moss and lichen. Then ferns take root; and, in the water-softened bark of the dead tree, seedlings of bigger trees spring up as a slowly developing forest in miniature. A twenty-year-old spruce might be only a foot high, yet its roots may have to go down twenty or thirty feet to reach the ground. Once it "pegs in," however, the tree shoots up, reaching its full height in about one hundred and fifty years.

A tree may live as long as eight hundred years, and it may be as many years again before all traces of it have disappeared. Nearly all the trees in the forest have begun life as seedlings on "nurse" logs and, in one of the remarkable features of the rain forest, have grown to create long and grand colonnades. At first the rain forest seems as haphazard as any jungle, but one soon realizes that each tree aligns perfectly with several of its neighbors. Often one can sight, through tunnels below, the arched roots of several trees in succession, showing where the nurse log they shared has completely rotted away.

Every tree soon collects its own colony of mosses, lichens and ferns, called epiphytes because they are supported by other plants. One tree can carry as many as forty species of these delicate plants.

The imagination can run riot in a place such as this, yet the forest is neither oppressive nor frightening. It is mysterious but not ghostly, damp but not chilling. It is silent—yet alive with faint whispers.

John Dyson

In Quest of a President

Every four years, Americans go to the polls to elect a President and Vice President. For many voters, the choice is simply a matter of deciding between the Democrats and the Republicans. Although third parties have surfaced from time to time—Theodore Roosevelt's Bull Moose, which split from the GOP in 1912, for example, and George Wallace's American Independent Party in 1968—American national politics still work basically within the two-party system.

The two-party tradition goes back to the early years of the nation's history. Although the Founding Fathers were suspicious of parties and even ignored them altogether in drafting the Constitution, Americans formed political alliances in the late 1700s to win elections and influence the policies of the government.

In 1796, George Washington had refused to run for a third term, so the election that year was a party contest between a Federalist, John Adams, and a Democratic-Republican, Thomas Jefferson.

By the end of Washington's administration, there were two fairly well defined political groups in the country. The Federalists, including Washington, Hamilton, Adams and their supporters, were nationalist in their outlook and favored a strong federal government. The Anti-Federalists, led by Thomas Jefferson and his supporters, tended to be more isolationist and favored less activity by the federal government.

In the years that followed, parties developed as Democratic-Republicans (later Democrats) and National Republicans, from 1769 to 1815; Democrats and Whigs, from 1835 to 1852; and Democrats and Republicans, from 1854 until today.

Political parties act somewhat as "brokers" who help to translate the wishes of the people into government policy. Parties help to explain complex issues, and they bring a kind of necessary order to the chaotic process of choosing among a multitude of candidates. Through primary elections, caucuses and conventions, party members decide which candidates to endorse in the general election, and they help to narrow the choice for the voting public.

A major political party must attract as many voters as possible. So parties are built on a broad philosophical base, and their platforms must appeal to a great variety of voters. Differences in the two major American parties seem to center around political philosophy. Republicans are generally considered to be more conservative; their platform in 1976, for instance, focused on reduced federal spending, more local control, and less governmental interference in the economy. That same year the Democratic platform favored greater use of the government's powers to promote full employment, relieve poverty and enforce civil rights legislation.

The final vote for the Presidency comes from the Electoral College, a concept dating back to 1787 when the Founding Fathers were drafting the Constitution. Debating how a President should be chosen, they decided that each state would choose wise and educated men to vote for all the people. The groups of electors came to be known as the Electoral College.

Political parties began to form by the election of 1796, and they took on the job of nominating presidential candidates. Electors were presented with party-supported candidates to choose from, and gradually more and more people were allowed to vote.

By 1828, in all but two of the twenty-four states, the electors were chosen by popular elections rather than state legislatures. Each party named electors who would vote for its presidential candidate, and the electors of the winning party almost automatically cast the state's electoral votes for their party's candidate.

The choice of a President has come closer to the common people than the Founding Fathers had intended. Although the Electoral College is considered to be an echo of the voice of the people, the concept has been criticized through the years, and various suggestions have been advanced for correcting its faults. Changing the structure of the College would require a Constitutional amendment, however.

Selected party members, or delegates, gather from all over the country every four years to attend the national conventions that serve four basic needs: to nominate the two top candidates, to adopt a national party platform, to govern the party, and to serve as an exciting, enthusiastic campaign rally.

The Presidency has grown so complex that a good many people wonder if any mortal can adequately fill the office. Nonetheless, the quest for this "splendid misery" reaches its culmination every four years in the national conventions where two men are singled out for the highest offices in the land.

Few of the thirty-eight former Presidents, however, had anything good to say about the office. Thomas Jefferson commented, "Never did a prisoner released from his chains feel such relief as I shall on shaking off the shackles of power." Truman remarked that "Being a President is like riding a tiger. A man has to keep riding or be swallowed." And Gen. William Tecumseh Sherman, who soundly resisted a "Draft Sherman" movement, made this sharp comment: "If forced to choose between the penitentiary and the White House for four years, I would say the penitentiary, thank you."

This year, the Republicans will hold their convention during the week of July 14 in Detroit. Democrats will gather at Madison Square Garden in New York City beginning August 11.

Republican delegates and their families can savor Detroit's historic flavor. The city was settled in 1701 by the French and named "d'etroit" or city "of straits," a reference to the twenty-seven-mile Detroit River that connects Lakes Erie and St. Clair. Belle Isle, an island park in the middle of the river, offers visitors an Aquarium, a Children's Zoo, and an Urban Nature Center.

Renaissance Center, a new civic center complex on the riverfront, is the largest privately financed development in the country. Although Detroit is thought of as the "Motor City," there are attractions other than those connected with the manufacture of automobiles. Many points of interest reflect Detroit's maritime connection, such as Old Mariner's Church and the Dossin Great Lakes Museum of Belle Isle.

Convention-goers can choose from several fine restaurants along the river or atop sky-high revolving rooftops downtown. Good ethnic restaurants offer Greek and Chinese food; some delegates might choose to eat, appropriately enough, at the Caucus Club.

Nearby Dearborn is a feast of American history. Greenfield Village offers Historic Houses, Suwanee Park and Island, the Thomas A. Edison Buildings and the Village Green. The Henry Ford Museum in Dearborn features the American Decorative Arts Galleries, Henry Ford Exhibits, Mechanical Arts Hall, and memorabilia in the Street of Early American Shops.

When the Democrats get together in the Big Apple in August, they'll find such an overwhelming variety of diversions that the choices are staggering. The three-hundred-foot-high Statue of Liberty, dominating the approach to the city's harbor, has been welcoming the "huddled masses yearning to breathe free" since 1885.

New York is a city of spectacular museums. The American Museum of Natural History is the largest in the world, with more than forty acres of floor space. The Whitney holds a vast collection of contemporary art; the Metropolitan Museum houses a collection of more than a million art objects that span the entire five thousand years of civilized human culture, and the Cloisters at Fort Tyron Park offer a splendid collection of medieval art. The Guggenheim, designed by Frank Lloyd Wright, holds a permanent collection of more than four thousand works of modern art.

Delegates will be awed by New York's skyscraper skyline—the Empire State Building, the art-deco style Chrysler Building, Rockefeller Center, the United Nations Building, and the twin towers of the 1302-foot tall World Trade Center. When the day's convention business is finished, the lights of Broadway will lead visitors to the best in legitimate American theater.

In both cities, after the applause and the balloons and the speeches and the hoopla, delegates will nominate their party's candidates.

Bea Bourgeois

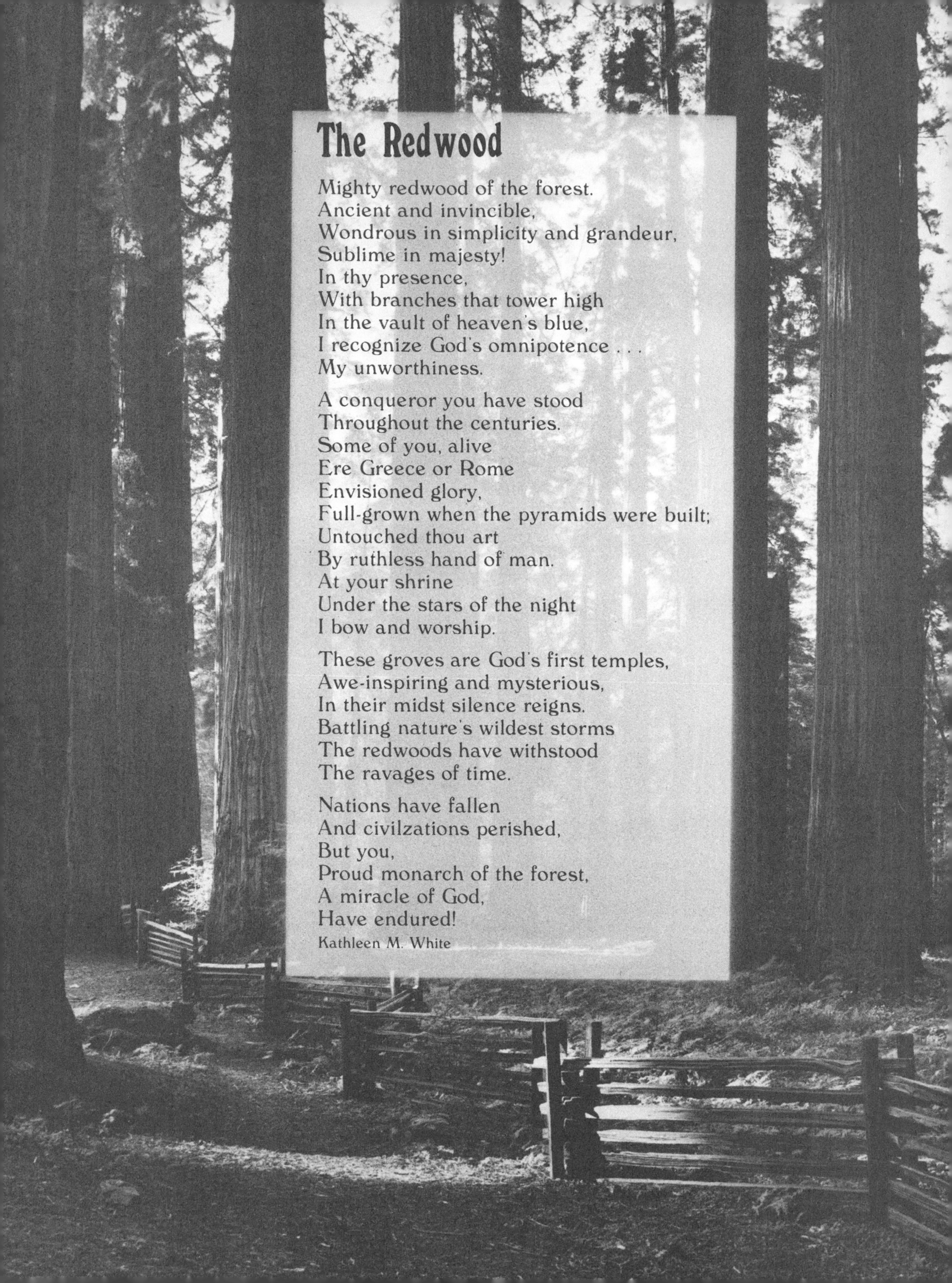

The Redwood

Mighty redwood of the forest.
Ancient and invincible,
Wondrous in simplicity and grandeur,
Sublime in majesty!
In thy presence,
With branches that tower high
In the vault of heaven's blue,
I recognize God's omnipotence . . .
My unworthiness.

A conqueror you have stood
Throughout the centuries.
Some of you, alive
Ere Greece or Rome
Envisioned glory,
Full-grown when the pyramids were built;
Untouched thou art
By ruthless hand of man.
At your shrine
Under the stars of the night
I bow and worship.

These groves are God's first temples,
Awe-inspiring and mysterious,
In their midst silence reigns.
Battling nature's wildest storms
The redwoods have withstood
The ravages of time.

Nations have fallen
And civilzations perished,
But you,
Proud monarch of the forest,
A miracle of God,
Have endured!

Kathleen M. White

The sunshine falls in glory through the colossal spires and crowns, each a symbol of health and strength, the noble shafts faithfully upright like pillars of temples, upholding a roof of infinite, leafy, inter-lacing arches and fretted skylights.

John Muir

Redwood Sentinels

I feel their iron bark and know
These redwoods stand to testify
That long after man has known his day
Their lofty arms will brush the sky.

Their branches meet above my head,
Where silent, dusky green
Of shadows and the sigh of winds
Are lonely and serene.

I make a prayer to God
To praise his plan:
How tall, the redwood . . .
How small is man.

Helen Virden

Isles of the Sea

Agnes Davenport Bond

Isles of the sea,
Isles of the sea,
Today, they are
Fresh in my memory,
A land of romance,
Where beauty lies,
Under the clearest
Of sapphire skies,
Where the scent is sweet
Of Hawaiian flowers,
And the sunlight streams
Through the fitful showers.
And the salty tang
Of the ocean sweeps.
Here lavishly bloom
All shrubs and trees;
And fragrance is wafted
On the breeze.
A country of color,
Of splendor, and thrills,
Of seashore and mountains,
Of valleys and hills.

How enchanting these crossroads
Far out on the sea!
And their lure of adventure
Is calling me.
I want to go back
To Aloha land,
And lie again
On the sea-washed sand,
And to hear again,
At the channel buoy,
The sweet, sad strains
Of "Aloha Oe."
Isles of the sea,
Isles of the sea,
Treasured today
In my memory.

Alaska Highway

The 1,422-mile Alaska Highway is the only road connecting Alaska with Canadian and United States road systems. Built during World War II as a military supply route, the highway cost $140 million and has a mostly gravel surface.

Eiffel Tower

Designed for the 1889 exposition by Gustave Eiffel, the Eiffel Tower rises 984 feet above the city of Paris. About 6,400 metric tons of iron and steel make up the tower, which houses restaurants, elevators, areas for experimentation and a weather station.

The Seven Wonders
of the

Golden Gate Bridge

Joseph B. Strauss designed the 8,981-foot-long Golden Gate Bridge, which connects northern California to the peninsula of San Francisco. This spectacular suspension bridge, containing a six-lane road and sidewalks, is supported by two cables, 36½ inches in diameter.

R. Adair

Dneproges Dam

The Dneproges Dam on the Dnepr River supplies hydroelectric power for a majority of southern Russia's mines and industries. The 5,000-foot-long concrete structure holds back 1,600,000 cubic yards of water used to generate 650,000 kilowatts of electricity.

Empire State Building

New York City's Empire State Building rises 1,472 feet, including 102 stories and a television tower. The fifty-year-old skyscraper houses about 10,000 tenants and has over 1½ million visitors annually.

Atomic Energy Research Establishment

Modern World

One of the world's major scientific laboratories is the Atomic Energy Research Establishment at Harwell, England. Experimental facilities, including several large particle accelerators and six research reactors, enable researchers to study all aspects of atomic energy.

Suez Canal

The man-made Suez Canal waterway in Egypt extends nearly 100 miles across the Isthmus of Suez, joining the Mediterranean and Red seas. The canal has been widened and deepened several times since its construction in 1869. Currently 46 feet deep and 390 feet wide at the surface, the canal is, for the most part, limited to one-lane traffic.

PHOTOS THAT SAY, "LOOK AT ME"

Successful photography depends upon more than technique, for another requirement is an awareness of aesthetics. Great photographs depend more upon the principles of beauty than they do upon a mastery of the technical aspects of photography. What is the main difference between a mere snapshot and an outstanding photo? An understanding of the answer to this question can help make travel pictures a joy for all to behold.

Let us suppose someone were to travel to Hawaii and take a picture at the beach. What would the photo look like? Would it contain a hodgepodge of sunbathers lying about the beach in helter-skelter fashion, with palm trees jutting in and out of the picture? If so, it would be an example of one of the capital sins of aesthetics: disorganization. In order to become meaningful, the various elements of a photograph should not be brought together in an entirely arbitrary manner, but should be arranged into a harmonious whole. For an example of a photograph which is carefully organized and illustrates some of the basic axioms of good composition, let us take a look at the photo on the opposite page.

First of all, the elements of this travel picture are arranged in a meaningful way. The picture seems to shout, "Hawaii," for one glimpse is all that is needed to discern its location. Everything one needs to know in order to identify the locale is there: Diamond Head, palm trees, blue sky and ocean, beach and bathers, sailboats and hotels. And yet, the photo is not at all crowded.

This brings us to our second principle of good pictures: simplicity. It is generally true that the smaller the number of elements in a picture, the better. The trick is to use just enough elements to deliver your message. Of course, if you want to show how crowded a particular beach may be, include plenty of people, but do not include anything irrelevant. The rule of simplicity extends to design and color. In other words, the simpler the design and the fewer the colors, the better the picture will be, except of course, when the theme specifically deals with complexity of design or color.

The next design element is as simple as they come: framing the subject. Note how the innermost trees frame Diamond Head, the boats, and the first couple; next, how the pair of trees on the right frame the standing couple. At the same time, the outermost trees serve as a border, unifying all of the elements to form a single meaningful picture.

Another attribute of the photograph is balance. In the foreground, there are four trees and four people, and both trees and people are divided into groups of two. In addition to this rhythmical repetition of elements, the position of the horizon also affects the overall balance of the picture. A successful scenic usually has a high or low horizon, and the picture grows increasingly less appealing as the horizon approaches the exact center of the composition.

Still another characteristic of all good pictures is mood. That is, the ability to convey an emotion. What emotion or mood does our example photo communicate, and how do the various elements of the picture help deliver the message? The mood is tranquility. Note how this feeling seems to permeate the scene: both couples are at rest, the boats are moored; there are no strong waves visible; the palm leaves seem to indicate the absence of any wind. In other words, the scene is full of inactivity.

Additionally, the long shadows of the trees hint that it is nearing the end of the day, a time of rest. Again, the predominant color is blue, which psychologically conveys the feeling of peace. Finally, because the mere name "Hawaii" conjures up an image of a place to relax, the very elements which identify the location of the photograph assist in conveying the mood of tranquility.

Although these many points are not obvious at the conscious level of our minds, they are nevertheless picked up by the subconscious (the seat of our emotions), and are thereby worthy of consideration. The lesson is clear: for better travel pictures, think before you shoot; take time to organize.

Chuck Gallozzi

Article and photograph opposite
Courtesy of *Photo Life* Magazine
For subscription information
Write 230 - 144 Front Street West
Toronto, Ontario M5J 1G2

Around the World in Eighty Days

Jules Verne

This abridged version has been prepared
especially for Ideals
by Norma Barnes

Mr. Phileas Fogg lived, in 1872, at No. 7, Saville Row, Burlington Gardens. . . . Was [he] rich? Undoubtedly. But those who knew him best could not imagine how he had made his fortune. . . . He was . . . the least communicative of men. . . . His daily habits were quite open to observation; but whatever he did was so exactly the same thing that he had always done before that the wits of the curious were fairly puzzled.

Phileas Fogg was not known to have either wife or children, . . . relatives or near friends. . . . He lived alone in his house in Saville Row. . . . The mansion, though not sumptuous, was exceedingly comfortable. . . .

. . .

A rap . . . sounded on the door . . . A young man of thirty advanced and bowed. "You are a Frenchman, I believe," asked Phileas Fogg.

"Jean Passepartout, . . ." replied the newcomer.

"You are well recommended to me; I hear a good report of you. . . . What time is it?" Mr. Fogg asked.

"Twenty-two minutes after eleven," returned Passepartout, drawing an enormous silver watch from the depths of his pocket.

"You are too slow," said Mr. Fogg.

"Pardon me, Monsieur, it is impossible—"

"You are four minutes too slow. No matter; it's enough to mention the error. Now from this moment, twenty-nine minutes after eleven A.M., this Wednesday, October 2, you are in my service."

. . .

A Daring Wager

Several members of the Reform Club came in and drew up to the fireplace, where a coal fire was steadily burning. They were Mr. Fogg's usual partners at whist . . . , all rich and highly respectable personages.

"Well, Ralph," said Thomas Flanagan, "what about that robbery?"

"I hope we may put our hands on the robber. Skillful detectives have been sent to all the principal ports of America and the Continent, and he'll be a clever fellow if he slips through their fingers."

"But have you got the robber's description?" asked Stuart.

"In the first place, he is no robber at all," returned Ralph, positively. . . .

"The *Daily Telegraph* says that he is a gentleman."

It was Phileas Fogg, whose head now emerged from behind his newspaper, who made this remark. He bowed to his friends and entered into the conversation . . .

There were real grounds for supposing, as the *Daily Telegraph* said, that the thief did not belong to a professional band. On the day of the robbery a well-dressed gentleman of polished manners, with a well-to-do air, had been observed going to and fro in the paying-room, where the crime was committed.

"I maintain," said Stuart, "that the chances are in favor of the thief, who must be a shrewd fellow."

"Well, but where can he fly to?" asked Ralph. "No country is safe for him."

"Pshaw!"

"Oh, I don't know that. The world is big enough."

"It was once," said Phileas Fogg, in a low tone.

. . . "What do you mean by 'once'? Has the world grown smaller?"

"Certainly," returned Ralph. "I agree with Mr. Fogg. The world has grown smaller, since a man can now go round it ten times more quickly than a hundred years ago."

"In eighty days," interrupted Phileas Fogg.

. . . "I'd like to see you do it in eighty days. . . . I would wager four thousand pounds that such a journey . . . is impossible. . . ."

. . ."All right," said Mr. Fogg and, turning to the others, he continued, "I have a deposit of twenty thousand at Baring's which I will willingly risk upon it. . . . Do you accept?"

"We accept," replied Messrs. Stuart, Fallentin, Sullivan, Flanagan, and Ralph, after consulting each other.

A Beginning

. . . By eight o'clock Passepartout had packed the modest carpetbag containing the wardrobes of his master and himself; then, still troubled in mind, he carefully shut the door of his room, and descended to Mr. Fogg.

. . .

Mr. Fogg and his servant seated themselves in a first-class carriage at twenty minutes before nine; five minutes later the whistle screamed, and the train slowly glided out of the station. . .

A Suspicion

. . . The commissioner of police was sitting in his office at nine o'clock one evening, when the following telegraphic dispatch was put into his hands:

Suez to London

Rowan, Commissioner of Police, Scotland Yard: I've found the bank robber, Phileas Fogg. Send without delay warrant of arrest to Bombay.

Fix, Detective

The mysterious habits of Phileas Fogg were recalled; his solitary ways, his sudden departure; and it seemed clear that, in undertaking a tour round the world on the pretext of a wager, he had had no other end in view than to elude the detectives and throw them off his track.

. . .

A Dubious Friendship

Detective Fix joined Passepartout, who was lounging and looking about on the quay. . . . "Well, my friend . . . you are looking about you?"

"Yes, but we travel so fast that I seem to be journeying in a dream."

"You are in a great hurry, then?"

"I am not, but my master is . . . Above all," said Passepartout, "don't let me lose the steamer."

"You have plenty of time; it's only twelve o'clock."

Passepartout pulled out his big watch. "Twelve!" he exclaimed. "Why it's only eight minutes before ten."

"Your watch is slow."

"My watch? It doesn't vary five minutes in the year; it's a perfect chronometer."

"I see how it is," said Fix. "You have kept London time, which is two hours behind that of Suez. You ought to regulate your watch at noon in each country."

"I regulate my watch? Never!"

"Well, then, it will not agree with the sun."

"So much the worse for the sun, Monsieur. The sun will be wrong, then!" And the worthy fellow returned the watch to its fob with a defiant gesture.

. . . Passepartout and Fix got into the habit of chatting together, the latter making it a point to gain the worthy man's confidence, [the unsuspecting] Passepartout, mentally pronouncing Fix the best of good fellows.

. . . What was Phileas Fogg doing all this time? He made his four hearty meals every day, regardless of the most persistent rolling and pitching on the part of the steamer; and he played whist indefatigably. . . .

The Journey Continues

. . . The *Mongolia* was due at Bombay on the 22nd; she arrived on the 20th. This was a gain to Phileas Fogg of two days since his departure from London, and he calmly entered the fact in the itinerary, in the columns of gains.

The passengers of the *Mongolia* went ashore at half-past four P.M.; at exactly eight the train would start for Calcutta.

. . .

A Heroic Adventure

. . . The train stopped, at eight o'clock, in the midst of a glade some fifteen miles beyond Rothal, where there were several bungalows and workmen's cabins. The conductor, passing along the carriages, shouted, "Passengers will get out here!" . . .

. . . The railway came to a termination at this point. The papers [it seemed] were like some watches, which have a way of getting too fast, and had been premature in their announcement of the completion of the line. . . .

. . .

Mr. Fogg and Sir Francis Cromarty, after searching the village from end to end, came back without having found any means of conveyance.

"I shall go afoot," said Phileas Fogg.

Passepartout had been looking about him and, after a moment's hesitation, said, "Monsieur, I think I have found our means of conveyance."

"What?"

"An elephant! An elephant that belongs to an Indian who lives but a hundred steps from here."

"Let's go and see the elephant," replied Mr. Fogg. . . .

Phileas Fogg proposed to purchase the animal outright, [and] at two thousand pounds the Indian yielded.

"What a price, good heaven!" cried Passepartout, "for an elephant!"

. . . At two o'clock the [party] entered a thick forest which extended several miles; [the guide] preferred to travel under cover of the woods. They had not as yet had any unpleasant encounters, and the journey seemed on the point of being successfully accomplished, when the elephant, becoming restless, suddenly stopped.

"A procession of Brahmans is coming this way. We must prevent their seeing us, if possible." . . .

. . . Some Brahmans, [were approaching] clad in all the sumptuousness of Oriental apparel, and leading a woman who faltered at every step. This woman was young, and as fair as a European. Her head and neck, shoulders, ears, arms, hands, and toes, were loaded down with jewels and gems, with bracelets, earrings, and rings. . . .

. . . Sir Francis watched the procession with a sad countenance, and, turning to the guide, said, "A suttee."

The Parsee nodded, and put his finger to his lips. . . .

. . . Phileas Fogg had heard what Sir Francis said, and, as soon as the procession had disappeared, asked, "What is a 'suttee'?"

"A suttee," returned the general, "is a human sacrifice, but a voluntary one. The woman you have just seen will be burned tomorrow at the dawn of day."

"And the corpse?" asked Mr. Fogg.

"Is that of the prince, her husband," said the guide; "an independent Raja of Bundelcund." . . .

. . . The guide shook his head several times, and now said, "The sacrifice which will take place tomorrow at dawn is not a voluntary one."

"How do you know?"

"Everybody knows about this affair in Bundelcund."

"But the wretched creature did not seem to be making any resistance," observed Sir Francis.

"That was because they had intoxicated her with fumes of hemp and opium" . . .

. . . Mr. Fogg stopped him, and, turning to Sir Francis Cromarty, said, "Suppose we save this woman."

"Save the woman, Mr. Fogg!"

"I have yet twelve hours to spare; I can devote them to that."

"Why, you are a man of heart!"

"Sometimes," replied Phileas Fogg, quietly, "when I have the time." . . .

. . .

The hours passed, and the lighter shades now announced the approach of day, though it was not yet light. This was the moment.

Phileas Fogg and his companions mingled in the rear ranks of the crowd; and in two minutes they reached the banks of the stream and stopped fifty paces from the pyre, upon which still lay the raja's corpse. In the semi-obscurity they saw the victim, quite senseless, stretched out beside her husband's body. Then a torch was brought, and the wood, soaked with oil, instantly took fire.

At this moment Sir Francis and the guide seized Phileas Fogg, who, in an instant of mad generosity, was about to rush upon the pyre. But he had quickly pushed them aside, when the whole scene suddenly changed. A cry of terror arose. The whole multitude prostrated themselves, terror-stricken, on the ground.

The old raja was not dead, then, since he rose of a sudden, like a specter, took up his wife in his arms, and descended from the pyre in the midst of the clouds of smoke, which only heightened his ghostly appearance.

continued

It was Passepartout who had . . . slipped upon the pyre . . . and delivered the young woman from death.

A moment after, all four of the party had disappeared in the woods, and the elephant was bearing them away at a rapid pace. But the cries and the noise, and a ball which whizzed through Phileas Fogg's hat, apprised them that the trick had been discovered.

The old raja's body, indeed, now appeared upon the pyre; and the priests, recovered from their terror, perceived that an abduction had taken place. They hastened into the forest, followed by the soldiers, who fired a volley after the fugitives; but the latter rapidly increased the distance between them, and ere long found themselves beyond the reach of the bullets and arrows.

. . . Soon after, Phileas Fogg, Sir Francis Cromarty, and Passepartout, were installed in a carriage with Aouda (the young woman whom they had rescued). . . .

Phileas Fogg . . . offered . . . to escort her to Hong Kong, where she might remain safely until the affair was hushed up—an offer which she eagerly and gratefully accepted. She had a relation, who was one of the principal merchants of Hong Kong, . . .

A Gracious Offer

[In Hong Kong] Mr. Fog repaired to the Exchange, where, he made the inquiry, only to learn that [Aouda's relative] had left China two years before, and, retiring from business with an immense fortune, had taken up his residence in Europe—in Holland, the broker thought.

Aouda at first said nothing. she passed her hand across her forehead, and reflected a few moments. Then, in her sweet, soft voice, she said, "What ought I to do, Mr. Fogg?"

"It is very simple," responded the gentleman. "Go on to Europe."

Across a Vast Continent

. . . On the 3rd of December, the "General Grant" entered the bay of the Golden Gate and reached San Francisco.

Mr. Fogg had neither gained nor lost a single day.

. . . The train left Oakland station at six o'clock. It was already night, cold and cheerless, the heavens being overcast with clouds which seemed to threaten snow.

. . . About twelve o'clock, a troup of ten or twelve thousand head of buffalo encumbered the track. The locomotive, slackening its speed, tried to clear the way with its cowcatcher; but the mass of animals was too great. The buffaloes marched along with a tranquil gait, uttering now and then deafening bellowings. There was no use in interrupting them, for, having taken a particular

direction, nothing can moderate and change their course; it is a torrent of living flesh which no dam could contain.

. . . The train pursued its course, without interruption.

. . . Suddenly savage cries resounded in the air, accompanied by reports which certainly did not issue from the car where [they] were. The reports continued in front and the whole length of the train. Cries of terror proceeded from the interior of the cars.

Colonel Proctor and Mr. Fogg, revolvers in hand, . . . rushed forward where the noise was most clamorous. They then perceived that the train was attacked by a band of Sioux.

The Sioux were armed with guns, from which came the reports, to which the passengers, who were almost all armed, responded by revolver shots.

Fort Kearney station, where there was a garrison, was only two miles distant; but that once passed, the Sioux would be masters of the train between Fort Kearney and the station beyond.

[The train continued to roll.] The conductor was fighting beside Mr. Fogg, when he was shot and fell. At the same moment he cried, "Unless the train is stopped in five minutes, we are lost!"

"Stay, Monsieur," said Passepartout; "I will go."

Carried on by the force already acquired, the train still moved for several minutes; but the brakes were worked, and at last they stopped, less than a hundred feet from Kearney station.

The soldiers of the fort, attracted by the shots, hurried up; the Sioux had not expected them, and decamped in a body before the train entirely stopped.

. . .

Phileas Fogg found himself twenty hours behind time. He examined a curious vehicle, a kind of frame on two long beams, a little raised in front like the runners of a sledge, and upon which there was room for five or six persons. . . .

What a journey! The travellers, huddled close together, could not speak for the cold, intensified by the rapidity at which they were going. . . .

A train was ready to start when Mr. Fogg and his party reached the station, and they only had time to get into the cars.

. . . At last the Hudson came into view; and at a quarter-past eleven in the evening of the 11th, the train stopped in the station on the right bank of the river, before the very pier of the Cunard line.

The "China," for Liverpool, had started three quarters of an hour before!

A Mutiny

[Phileas Fogg] seemed about to give up all hope, when he espied a trading vessel getting ready for departure. . . .

"Will you carry me and three other persons to Liverpool?"

"No! I am setting out for Bordeaux. . . ."

"Well, will you carry me to Bordeaux?"

"No, not if you paid me two hundred dollars."

"I offer you two thousand."

"Apiece?"

"Apiece."

. . . "I start at nine o'clock," said Captain Speedy, simply. . . . .

"We will be on board at nine o'clock," replied, no less simply, Mr. Fogg.

. . . They were on board when the "Henrietta" made ready to weigh anchor. . . .

At noon the next day . . . Captain Speedy . . . was shut up in his cabin under lock and key. . . .

Phileas Fogg wished to go to Liverpool, but the captain would not carry him there. . . . [So he] had so shrewdly managed with his banknotes that the sailors and stokers . . . went over to him in a body. . . .

On the 18th of December, the engineer . . . announced that the coal would give out in the course of the day.

. . .

"I have sent for you, [Captain]," continued Mr. Fogg, "to ask you to sell me your vessel."

"No! By all the devils, no!"

"But I shall be obliged to burn her."

"Burn the 'Henrietta'!"

"Yes; at least the upper part of her. The coal has given out."

"Burn my vessel!" cried Captain Speedy, who could scarcely pronounce the words. "A vessel worth fifty thousand dollars!"

"Here are sixty thousand," replied Phileas Fogg.

. . .

Phileas Fogg at last disembarked on the Liverpool quay, at twenty minutes before twelve, December 21st. He was only six hours distant from London.

The Final Delay

But at this moment Fix came up, put his hand upon Mr. Fogg's shoulder, and, showing his warrant, said, "You are really Phileas Fogg?"

"I am."

"I arrest you in the Queen's name!"

Phileas Fogg was in prison. He had been shut up in the Custom House, and he was to be transferred to London the next day.

The Custom House clock struck one. Mr. Fogg observed that his watch was two hours too fast.

Two hours! Admitting that he was at this moment taking an express train, he could reach London and the Reform Club by a quarter before nine, p.m. His forehead slightly wrinkled.

The door swung open, and he saw Passepartout, Aouda, and Fix, who hurried towards him.

Fix was out of breath, and his hair was in disorder. He could not speak. "Sir," he stammered, "Sir—forgive me—a most-unfortunate resemblance—robber arrested three days ago—you—are free!"

Phileas Fogg was free!

Phileas Fogg then ordered a special train.

But . . . when Mr. Fogg stepped from the train at the terminus, all the clocks in London were striking ten minutes before nine.

Having made the tour of the world, he was behindhand five minutes. He had lost the wager!

All Is Lost?

Phileas Fogg returned home . . . took a chair, and sat down near the fireplace, opposite Aouda. No emotion was visible on his face. Fogg returned was exactly the Fogg who had gone away; there was the same calm, the same impassibility.

He sat several minutes without speaking; then, bending his eyes on Aouda, "Madam," said he, "will you pardon me for bringing you to England?"

"I, Mr. Fogg!" replied Aouda, checking the pulsations of her heart.

"Please let me finish," returned Mr. Fogg. "When I decided to bring you far away from the country which was so unsafe for you, I was rich, and counted on putting a portion of my fortune at your disposal; then your existence would have been free and happy. But now I am ruined. . . ."

"Mr. Fogg," said Aouda, rising, and seizing his hand, "do you wish at once a kinswoman and friend? Will you have me for your wife?"

Mr. Fogg shut his eyes for an instant, as if to avoid her look. When he opened them again, "I love you!" he said, simply. "Yes, by all that is holiest, I love you, and I am entirely yours!"

Passepartout was summoned.

. . .

A Victory

The five antagonists of Phileas Fogg had met in the great saloon of the club.

"Sixteen minutes to nine!" said John Sullivan, in a voice which betrayed his emotion.

One minute more, and the wager would be won.

At the fortieth second, nothing. At the fiftieth, still nothing.

At the fifty-fifth, a loud cry was heard in the street, followed by applause, hurrahs, and some fierce growls.

The players rose from their seats.

At the fifty-seventh second the door of the saloon opened; and the pendulum had not beat the sixtieth second when Phileas Fogg appeared, followed by an excited crowd who had forced their way through the club doors, and in his calm voice, said, "Here I am, gentlemen!"

Yes, Phileas Fogg in person.

The reader will remember that at five minutes past eight in the evening Passepartout had been sent by his master to engage the services of the Reverend Samuel Wilson.

He soon reached the clergyman's house, but found him not at home. Passepartout waited a good twenty minutes, and when he left the reverend gentleman, it was thirty-five minutes past eight. But in what a state he was!

Phileas Fogg had, without suspecting it, gained one day on his journey, and this merely because he had travelled constantly eastward; he would, on the contrary, have lost a day, had he gone in the opposite direction, that is, westward.

The Wealth of the World

That evening, Mr. Fogg, as tranquil as ever, said to Aouda, "Is our marriage still agreeable to you?"

"Mr. Fogg," replied she, "it is for me to ask that question. You were ruined, but now you are rich again."

"Pardon me, Madam; my fortune belongs to you."

What had he really gained by all this trouble? What had he brought back from this long and weary journey?

Nothing, say you? Perhaps so; nothing but a charming woman, who, strange as it may appear, made him the happiest of men!

Truly, would you not for less than that make the tour around the world?

Remember Paris? We savored petit fours
    At an outdoor café
And relaxed, inhaling the atmosphere.
    It was spring
And Paris had a lyrical loveliness,
    A loveliness almost ethereal . . .

Then we wandered along the Left Bank,
    Lingering at the Sorbonne and
Browsing through books and sketches
    Along the Boulevards Saint Michel
        And Saint Germain—
You bought me violets and held my hand,
    And we were alive with the wonder of Paris
        And ourselves . . .

One day we climbed up Montmartre,
    And there it was
The Cathedral of Sacre Coeur,
    Its white dome pink-gold in the sunset,
Imprinting itself upon us forever. . . .

We had a wonderful view of the city:
    The rooftops and lanes of Paris
Were before us—
    A palette of soft Utrillo colors

Remember Paris?

Lorice Fiani Mulhern

We strolled along the Champs Elysées
    In the shimmering sunlight
And kept falling in love with delightful Paris
    When, suddenly, it began to rain
        And thunder,
Melting trees and taxis and people together
    And arousing a symphony of discordant horns
Amid the driving slush and splatter.

One Sunday we sailed along the Seine,
    Marveling at the bridges and lamps
Of Paris (so many and so distinctive).
    We viewed the Cathedral of Notre Dame,
Hardly believing we were there—
    Remember?

Amid a scattering of treetops, chimneys
    And spires . . .
An artist nearby began folding his easel
    And a young boy walked along,
Playing his harmonica . . .

Such was Paris— Maxim's, the Louvre,
    The Eiffel Tower;
The sidewalk cafés athrong with people;
    The little side streets and shops,
The ride on the Metro . . .

All that fun and glamor,
    All that magnificent oldness and newness
Stirring and enrapturing us . . .
    Remember?

An Irish Mile

Maude Ludington Cain

Once, on a bright day, in a far, fairy isle,
I thought I would walk me an Irish mile—
An Irish mile was my morning desire,
So I took a gray road past a bog and a byre.
There was many a stone and many a stile,
But I would be going an Irish mile.
There were turf fires burning by benches, rough-hewn,
There was laughter, and lilt of an old Irish tune.
By sheep-cot and pen and a low, winding wall
I met an old grand'm with shillelagh and shawl;
I greeted a driver of donkey and cart,
To a blue-eyed colleen, sure, I near lost my heart.
And each spoke me cheery and gave me a smile
And bade me to tea and to rest for a while.
I heard barley sickles and smelled the ripe grain—
But never came I to the end of that lane.

Foot-weary at last and the sun going down
I came to a cottage close by to a town,
And said to a herder as I rested a while,
"Sure, 'tis long, friend, and long to the end of this mile."
He tipped his pipe ashes with a wave of his hand,
And replied, "Aye, it is that— but you understand
An Irish mile, darlin', is a mile and a bit—
And the bit, sure, is ever the most part of it . . ."
Oh, I can't be forgetting that slow Irish mile,
Where there's time for a chat and there's time for a smile;
Though on smooth roads and white roads I journey meanwhile
I fain would be going a far Irish mile—
A way-faring, gay-faring, sweet Irish mile.

Stonehenge: Monument of Mystery

Emmett Van Buskirk

Not far from Salisbury, England, and its great cathedral is the site of another imposing structure. On Salisbury Plain, Wiltshire, England, the massive stones of Stonehenge sit in majesty and mystery.

Stonehenge was probably built in several stages nearly four thousand years ago. Its construction occurred in what is referred to as the Neolithic Period (The New Stone Age). During this time man not only domesticated animals and plant forms, but also set aside and designed his own functional space in his world: established the beginnings of architecture. The materials used to construct many of these structures consisted of huge stones whose weight and size were so immense that the culture has been referred to as "megalithic." The name derives from the term "megalithic" given to describe the great stones.

I first saw Stonehenge one misty summer day, which only added to the mystery of this unique structure. My previous study did not prepare me for the awesome experience of walking among the massive stones. Even though there has been both natural and man-made destruction of the stones and their circular arrangement, the remains of Stonehenge still create an imposing sight.

Stonehenge is unique. There is nothing quite like it any other place in the world. Even from the earliest times visitors walked in amazement through the site and wondered at its construction and function just as I did.

Stonehenge is shaped in the form of a circle of huge stones known as a "cromlech." The outer boundary of this stone formation is a low, circular bank and ditch about one hundred feet from the stones. The building itself consisted of an outer ring of large stones capped by a lintel (crossbeam) stone. Inside this was a circle of smaller stones and an inner horseshoe of five upright

and lintel pairs. Standing separately from the other stones is one which is thought to mark the summer solstice, June 21.

Nearly four thousand years ago man created this extraordinary structure known as Stonehenge from huge stones, some of which approach fifty tons in weight and twenty feet in height. Stonehenge also exhibits refinements which do not occur elsewhere in some of the other early stone formations. Using stone hammers, men squared and dressed the stones, made accurate joints and fittings, and shaped the lintel stones into curves to fit their own segment of the circle. It is believed that the upright stones were carved with projecting knobs that rested in corresponding sockets on the cross stones. In addition, the stones in the outer circle of lintels are fitted to each other with tongue-and-groove joints.

The construction of Stonehenge on the open plain of southern England is even more amazing because there was no local source for the stones used. Some stones referred to as bluestones were probably brought from South Wales, mainly by water on rafts or boats. The route most likely taken involved a distance of nearly 240 miles. Some speculate that the transporting of the eighty-odd great stones which came from Marlborough Downs to Stonehenge overland may well have occupied a thousand men for several years. With rollers and sledge, the journey to Stonehenge and back with a single stone might have

taken two weeks. At the site on Salisbury Plain the upright stones were probably tipped carefully into foundation pits and packed. The horizontal lintels may have been set in place by being raised on a type of growing tower made from timbers.

Controversy still surrounds the purpose of Stonehenge. Some believe the design is that of an astronomical observatory which served as a remarkably accurate form of calendar.*

Whatever Stonehenge may be, the massive stones stand for each of us to walk among and ponder their silent strength and mystery.

*Gardner *Art Through the Ages*, 7th ed., Harcourt, Brace, Jovanovich, Inc. New York, 1980

Cathedral

From vaulted depths the towers rise and soar
In pinnacles and spires that pierce the blue,
So men may glimpse, in Gothic tracery,
Their prayer ascending to the infinite.
With upward gaze the heart attuned beholds
Imponderables carved in quarried stone,
While stained-glass radiance pours sacrament
On faith proclaimed aloft in ringing chimes.
In reverence the builders here have wrought
An affirmation of the spirit's quest;
An aspiration rendered visible—
The mortal thirst for immortality.

David B. Steinman

I believe in God—
this is a fine, praiseworthy thing to say.
But to acknowledge God,
wherever and however he manifests himself,
that in truth is heavenly bliss on earth.

J. W. Von Goethe

THE CALENDAR

Alfred Cohen

Without an organized calendar to count days, weeks, and years there would be no need for greeting cards. Without a calendar we could forget about bill paying at the end of the month because there would be no end of the month.

1 Primitive people didn't use calendars. Their lives were timed by the light of day and the dark of night. For most of them there was no need to measure time because they spent most of it as nomadic hunters. These ancients, though, were aware that the moon's phases never changed and that between

2 one full moon and the next there were about twenty-nine suns. As their nomadic tendencies declined in favor of a more stable, agrarian society, primitive people, spurred by a need to forecast planting times, developed methods for charting time. The moon's phases were chosen as a measuring device, the

7 days before the Nile began to crest. This observation gave them time to warn farmers to seek high ground before the bloated river reached their land. Over a fifty-year period records showed 365 days elapsed between two risings of Sirius. Egyptians were a sophisticated, civilized people 5000 years

8 ago, and among the most worldly wise was a physician named Troth. He was sufficiently influential to have his ideas about construction of a formal calendar accepted by the Pharaoh. Troth used the solar years of 365 days to build his calendar. Since planting time took place toward the end of Septem-

9 ber, the autumn equinox, Troth started each new year on what we know as September 23. Each month in the year contained thirty days and was identified by the numbers one through twelve, as were the days. Seven-day weeks were to come much later. Twelve months of thirty days each ac-

14 ing some old ideas and introducing new ones in an effort to regulate time spans in an orderly manner. Before Julius Caesar put his imprint on it, the Roman calendar was a mess, riddled by arbitrary exclusions and additions. As leader of the invading Roman legions as well as

15

Julius Caesar

16 Cleopatra's companion, Caesar spent considerable time in Egypt where he became familiar with the calendar developed by Troth. He was particularly drawn to its precise organization; and, assisted by Sosigenes, a Greek astronomer, Caesar proceeded to adopt the fundamental concepts

21
Caesar Augustus

22 so he ignored them. The power of the Roman Emperors was so absolute they could, with impunity, adjust important charts such as a calendar to suit their purposes, no matter how frivolous. Augustus followed Caesar as Rome's second Emperor. He felt the need to immortalize

23 himself in as many ways as possible. One of these was to rename the seventh month of the Julian calendar *August* to give himself parity with his esteemed predecessor. For good measure Augustus lopped one day off February and added it to his own month, giving August 31 days. In

28
FULL MOON

29 formed about the ten extra days, Pope Gregory propounded what has come to be called the "Gregorian Adjustment." The first part eliminated the bothersome ten days; Thursday, October 4, 1582, became Friday, October 15. The second part of the adjustment was more complex. It allowed

30 February twenty-eight days except in those years divisible by four—*leap years*—when it had twenty-nine. This rule does not apply to a *century* year such as 1600, 1700, 1800, 1900 and 2000 unless the century year divides by 400 equally. The year 1600 was a century leap year, as will

3

time between the full moons named *moonths*, a word which eventually became *months*. Theirs was an extremely primitive calendar for a primitive people. Credit the Egyptians with developing the concept of the first organized calendar. Its origins were rooted in the Nile River which, fed by melting

4

snows from the lofty plateaus of Central Africa, overflowed its banks two months of the year. During this time the Nile became a huge lake. When its waters receded, enormous mud flats were left behind which, despite the intense heat, retained enough moisture for people to engage in

5

LAST QUARTER

6

farming ten months of the year. The Egyptians began their calendar to keep track of and anticipate the Nile's flood stages. Again, the heavens provided the means for calculating, this time in the regular appearance of the fixed star Sirius. Temple priests noted that this star rose in the sky just a few

10

counted for 360 days, leaving 5¼ days left over. Extra days were placed at the end of the year and, unlike ordinary numbered days, were given names of five dieties worshiped at the Temple of Osiris. The remaining one-fourth day was handled this way, too, when it became a full day every

11

four years. Troth also broke up his calendar into smaller time units. Thirty days were subdivided into three ten-day groups. These days in turn were split into ten hours, each of which comprised 100 minutes, one minute equaling 100 seconds. The Egyptians liked to keep things orderly. Of

12

NEW MOON

13

the men who succeeded in restructuring the calendar Julius Caesar, Pope Gregory XIII, and Moses were perhaps the most influential. Moses' contribution was limited to one area. It was he who first proposed splitting a week into seven equal days. The other leaders rearranged the whole calendar, adapt-

17

of Troth's calendar. The only major change he made was the way he handled the five or six extra days that cropped up at the end of the year. On the Julian calendar, as it came to be known, these extra days were tacked on the ends of alternate months. Although opinions differ

18

about how the months came to be named—Quintilus was renamed July in honor of Caesar—the arrangement of the Julian calendar resembles our current calendar in many respects. Put into use about 46 B.C., it accounted for 365¼ days, pretty much the time it takes for the earth to travel

19

its orbit around the sun. But "pretty much" wasn't enough. To be precise Caesar's calendar was eleven minutes longer than the solar year on which it was constructed. Caesar decided he wouldn't be around when those eleven minutes added up over a couple of centuries,

20

FIRST QUARTER

24

Caesar's chart the number of days in a week (they were numbered, not named) varied between seven and eight, the arrival of market days determining the interval between weeks. Three centuries later Emperor Constantine tidied up the Julian calendar by a decree which declared each week

25

Moses

26

was to be exactly seven days long, an idea he presumably picked up from Moses. By 1582, during the reign of Pope Gregory XIII, the minutes accumulated under Caesar's calendar had become ten days, presenting the pontiff with a dilemma he solved very neatly. When he was in-

27

Pope Gregory XIII

31

be 2000. Sometime after the year 3000 an extra day will appear during the twelve month time frame, but it is presumed that calendar makers of the time will know what to do with it.

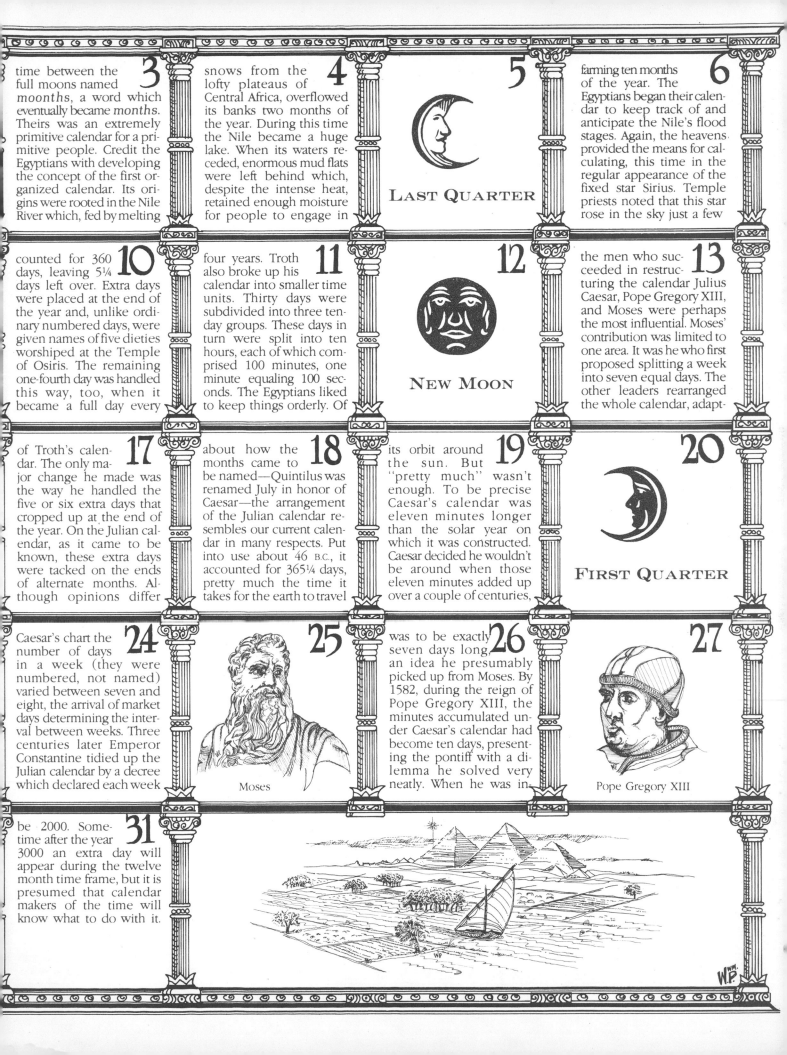

The mere mention of Switzerland calls up images of the incomparable Alps and picturesque chalets, their balconies overflowing with red geraniums. However, my favorite memories center around one city—Lucerne, capital of the canton of that name. Pictures spring to mind of two bridges and the figure of a lion sculptured in rock.

At the beginning of this century Lucerne was a small, quiet town, ideally situated on the River Reuss, which flows into beautiful Lake Lucerne. But it has now grown into a bustling city of approximately 80,000. During the tourist season it doubles in size.

Famous landmarks in Lucerne are two remarkable covered wooden bridges: the Kapellbrucke

day's sightseeing was a visit to the Lion of Lucerne." The Lion may be seen in the Glacier Gardens toward the outskirts of the city along the main road to Zurich. The Gardens received their name from the fact that they are located on the site of a moraine that dates from the Ice Age.

During excavations in 1852, geologists uncovered a natural grotto in which the Lowendenkmal, the famous Lion of Lucerne monument, carved from rock, now stands.

The paw of the suffering lion, mortally wounded by the arrow in his back, lies protectingly across the coat of arms of the French royal family. The figure was carved in memory

Images of Switzerland:

Lucerne's Painted Bridges

(Chapel Bridge) and the Spreuerbrucke (Mill Bridge), built in the fourteenth and fifteenth centuries, respectively, and profusely decorated with paintings. The Spreuerbrucke is famous for its painting of the "Death Dance" done by Caspar Meglinger from 1626 to 1632, and the Kapellbrucke for its series of scenes from Lucerne's history, painted by H. Wegmann on the gables—the full length of the bridge. Nearby is an ancient water tower, constructed about 1300, said to have served as a prison and torture chamber.

Both bridges are fascinating to visit, but, quoting from my diary, "The high point of the

of the Swiss guards who fought to the death in an attempt to defend Louis XVI when the Revolution broke out in 1792. The king escaped, but he gave no orders to his guards, caught like mice in a trap in the Tuileries. Hundreds were killed.

The work for this moving sculpture was done by Lucas Ahorn from the design of the famous Danish sculptor, Bertel Thorvaldsen, in 1820.

Although Thorvaldsen's work may be seen in widely scattered cities of the world, including Warsaw, Munich, Stuttgart, Cambridge, and the Vatican in Rome, the design for the Lion of Lucerne stands as one of his greatest—surely a perfect symbol of supreme sacrifice for a cause.

Doris A. Paul

Woodland Cathedral

Patience Strong

Go into the woodlands if you seek for peace of mind — at this time when Nature's mood is gentle, quiet and kind . . . When soft winds fan the trembling leaves about the cloistered glade — and paths go winding deep into the green and breathless shade.

Where nothing breaks the silence of the warm and fragrant air — but snatches of sweet melody . . . and wings that rend and tear — the stillness of the windless dells where shallow brooklets flow — and shadows fleck the water as the sunbeams come and go.

An unseen Presence walks the woods . . . A sense of holy things — haunts the dim Cathedral aisles; and every bird that sings — is like some morning chorister, and every breath of air — seems to bring the secret murmur of a whispered prayer.

©

On these pages
we are presenting a selection
from Vacation Ideals 1956.

In the Forest

Patience Strong

In the forest we can rise
above our worldly care;
in the forest we may find
tranquillity, and share
— the silence and the
secret strength of great
and ancient trees —
sturdy oaks and silver
birches, laughing in the
breeze.

In the forest we can learn
life's lessons if we will;
how to turn towards
the sunshine, standing
straight and still — how
to be content with slow
development — and grow,
in grace and strength in
spite of storms, of wind
and frost and snow . . .
Countless birds and in-
sects seek protection in
the tree — food and
shelter; isn't this true
hospitality? And when
winds have stripped the
branches of their sum-
mer dress — they survive
to show the world new
forms of loveliness.

Stately tree! Look down
on me — and teach me
how to be — Strong and
wise — To live my days
in quiet dignity . . . In
the forest silences our
petty warfares cease. In
God's own cathedral
we discover Truth and
Peace.

The Isles of Greece

The isles of Greece! The isles of Greece!
  Where burning Sappho loved and sung,
Where grew the arts of war and peace,
  Where Delos rose and Phoebus sprung!
Eternal summer gilds them yet,
But all, except their sun, is set.

The Scian and the Teian muse,
  The hero's harp, the lover's lute,
Have found the fame your shores refuse;
  Their place of birth alone is mute
To sounds which echo further west
Than your sires' "Islands of the Blest."

                  Lord Byron

We have received several requests from our readers asking for back issues of Ideals. With that in mind, we have listed the back issues of Ideals which are currently available. We trust this will allow you the opportunity to complete your personal library or order as a gift for any occasion. Write: Ideals Publishing Corporation, Dept. 105, 11315 Watertown Plank Rd., Milwaukee, Wisconsin 53226. Include just $3.00 for each title ordered. Postage and mailing will be included in this price.

SPECIAL HOLIDAY ISSUES

Christmas Ideals '78
Easter Ideals '79
Mother's Day Ideals '79
Thanksgiving Ideals '79
Christmas Ideals '79

POPULAR FAVORITES

Friendship Ideals '79
Carefree Days Ideals '79
Homespun Ideals '79
Autumn Ideals '79

Special Issue!

Ideals proudly presents a timely patriotic issue, *The Spirit of America*. It's filled with 64 pages of brilliant color photography, capturing the panoramic beauty of our land. Also included are poetry and prose reflecting our nation's spirit, feature articles on historical sites which mark our early struggle for freedom, and profiles of outstanding leaders of our country. A foreword by Senator William Proxmire explains why Americans should be proud of their country and of each other.

Send only $2.95 plus 30¢ postage and handling. (Wisconsin residents add 4% sales tax on total amount of books ordered.) Your copy of *The Spirit of America* will be sent promptly. Don't miss this special issue!

ACKNOWLEDGMENTS

THE PONY EXPRESS by Samuel Clemens. Excerpt from *Roughing It* (Harper & Row Publishers, Inc.). AVOCADO-CRAB DIP; LOBSTER NEWBURG; SEAFOOD CASSEROLE; SLIMMER CRAB CAKES. From *Ideals Fish and Seafood Cookbook* by Patricia Hansen, Copyright © 1979 by Howard Hansen. REMEMBER PARIS? by Lorice Fiani Mulhern. From *Realms of Enchantment* by Lorice Fiani Mulhern. Copyright © 1970 by Lorice Fiani Mulhern. Published by Dorrance & Company. By Robert Louis Stevenson: FAREWELL TO THE FARM; THE GARDENER; THE HAY-LOFT; THE VAGABOND. From *A Child's Garden of Verses* by Robert Louis Stevenson (Charles Scribner's Sons 1917). Our sincere thanks to the following authors whose addresses we were unable to locate: Maude Ludington Cain for AN IRISH MILE; Dick Diespecker for portions from BETWEEN TWO FURIOUS OCEANS; David B. Steinman for CATHEDRAL.

COLOR ART AND PHOTO CREDITS
(in order of appearance)

Front cover, Photo Media; inside front and back covers, Houses of Parliament and Big Ben, London, England, Colour Library International (USA) Limited; Windmill near Dennisport, Cape Cod, Massachusetts, Fred Sieb; THE SPIRIT OF AMERICA, John Slobodnik; HOMOSASSA JUNGLE IN FLORIDA, Winslow Homer, Fogg Art Museum; THE LAND OF EVANGELINE, Joseph Rusling Meeker, St. Louis Art Museum; Sculptured Rocks, the "Sugar Bowl" of the Lower Wisconsin Dells on Wisconsin River, Ken Dequaine; Poppies on mountainside, Banff National Park, Canada, Freelance Photographers Guild; The Little Brown Church in the Vale, Nashua, Iowa, Tracy Sweet; Baldwin's Crossing at Oak Creek Canyon, Arizona, Fred Sieb; Double arch formation in Arches National Park, Utah, Alpha Photo Associates; Totem Pole in Big Room, Carlsbad Caverns National Park, New Mexico, Josef Muench; Mount Grinnell and Grinnell Lake, Glacier National Park, Montana, Ed Cooper; Waterbuck, Colour Library International (USA) Limited; Bald eagle, Alaska Peninsula, Rollie Ostermick; Volcanic splendor, Wizard Island in Crater Lake at Crater Lake National Park, Oregon, Ken Dequaine; Washington Sol Duc Falls, Olympic National Park, Ed Cooper; Hibiscus, Hawaii state flower, Ed Cooper; Hawaiian splendor, Chuck Gallozzi; Pont Alexandre III and Eiffel Tower, Paris, France, Colour Library International (USA) Limited; Rock of Cashel, Tipperary County, Ireland, Colour Library International (USA) Limited; Castle Neuschwanstein in foothills of Bavarian Alps, Germany, Josef Muench; Village church of Lauterbrunnen in Lauterbrunnen Valley, Switzerland, Josef Muench; Temple of Zeus, Athens, Greece, Josef Muench; back cover, H. Armstrong Roberts.